OF MEN AND MONSTERS

TOM DEADY

Let the world know:
#IGotMyCLPBook!

Crystal Lake Publishing
www.CrystalLakePub.com

Copyright 2021 Tom Deady

Join the Crystal Lake community today
on our newsletter and Patreon!

All Rights Reserved

Cover Design:
Ben Baldwin—http://benbaldwin.co.uk/

Interior Layout:
Lori Michelle—www.theauthorsalley.com

Proofread by:
Hasse Chacon

This is a work of fiction. Names, characters, businesses, places, events and incidents are either the products of the author's imagination or used in a fictitious manner. Any resemblance to actual persons, living or dead, or actual events is purely coincidental.

No part of this publication may be reproduced, stored in a retrieval system, or transmitted in any form or by any means, without the prior permission in writing of the publisher, nor be otherwise circulated in any form of binding or cover than that in which it is published and without a similar condition including this condition being imposed on the subsequent purchaser.

Other Titles by the Author:

Haven
Eternal Darkness
Weekend Getaway
Backwater
Coleridge
Tales From Circadia

WELCOME
TO ANOTHER

CRYSTAL LAKE PUBLISHING
CREATION

Join today at www.crystallakepub.com & www.patreon.com/CLP

WELCOME TO ANOTHER CRYSTAL LAKE PUBLISHING CREATION.

Thank you for supporting independent publishing and small presses. You rock, and hopefully you'll quickly realize why we've become one of the world's leading publishers of Dark Fiction and Horror. We have some of the world's best fans for a reason, and hopefully we'll be able to add you to that list really soon.

To follow us behind the scenes (while supporting independent publishing and our authors), be sure to join our interactive community of authors and readers on Patreon (https://www.patreon.com/CLP) for exclusive content. You can even subscribe to all our future releases. Otherwise drop by our website and online store (www.crystallakepub.com/). We'd love to have you.

Welcome to Crystal Lake Publishing—Tales from the Darkest Depths.

Other Novellas by Crystal Lake Publishing:

The Pale White by Chad Lutzke
Quiet Places: A Novella of Cosmic Folk Horror
by Jasper Bark
Little Dead Red by Mercedes M. Yardley

For Sheila, as a new chapter of us begins . . .

JUNE 25, 1975

"THIS IS IT?" Matt asked.

Mom gave a harried sigh. "It doesn't look like much from the outside," she said, far too cheerily if you ask me, "but wait until you get in before you judge."

My brother mumbled something and pushed open the passenger-side door, groaning as he stretched.

Drama queen, I thought. I scrambled out of the back seat, and the cool sea breeze hit me. It smelled salty and fishy—and I loved it. On the enthusiasm meter, I was way closer to Mom than to Matt.

"What are we even going to do here?" He picked up a rock and tossed it lazily toward the beach.

"Are you kidding?" I cried, "the house is practically right on the water!"

"Yeah," Matt said with a glare, "and we don't know a single person, dildo."

"Matt! Watch your language."

He shrugged and shuffled toward the beach. I followed, keeping my distance.

"Take a quick look around, then come right back and help me unload," Mom called.

I waved to acknowledge her then jogged a few paces to catch up to my big brother as he crossed the empty street. We stepped over a chain that separated

1

TOM DEADY

the diagonal parking spaces from the beach. And that was it. Sand under our feet and waves crashing in front of us. I bent to pick up a cool shell, placing it in my pocket and keeping my eyes peeled for whatever other treasures might await me.

Matt had stopped just at the water's edge. I came up behind him as he stood motionless, staring out at nothing in particular.

"It might be kind of fun to live here," I said. I didn't think he was going to respond, but then he turned to me. He wasn't crying, but was pretty close. He wore his pain openly: lips tight, eyes narrow and wet. Then the corners of his lips moved. Not a smile, but something other than his grim expression of a moment ago.

"Yeah," he finally said. "Maybe."

He was only three years older than me, but the years between eleven and fourteen were longer than most. At least they seemed like it, to me. My brother was closer to being an adult than he was to being a kid. I looked up to him, but was in no hurry to get to where he was. I liked eleven just fine. Even without a father.

We walked back toward the house, carrying our sneakers and dragging our feet in the warm sand. I picked up a few more shells along the way.

At the end of the driveway, I stopped to examine the house. It was in rough shape; the merciless sea air had taken its toll. The washed-out paint, once some shade of blue, I guessed, had faded to a sad gray mess. The white trim was mostly chipped. The shutters were all broken or crooked, one swinging in the sharp breeze, banging against the house, then bouncing back the other way. *Home,* I thought, and trudged over to the car to grab something to carry in.

OF MEN AND MONSTERS

Mom was already unpacking a box of kitchen stuff and I heard Matt walking around upstairs.

"What've you got there, Ryan?" Without waiting for an answer, she peeled back the folded box cover and looked inside. "My bedroom," she said. "Top of the stairs, last door on the right."

I lugged the box up the creaky stairs, noticing every crack in the wall, every spot of peeling paint, every dirty smudge. I reached the top, realizing I was *looking* for negative things, looking at the house the way my brother does. *No more*, I thought. I shook my head and started down the hall. As I passed the first door on the left, gurgling water sounded on the other side of the door. *Bathroom*, I noted, and kept going toward Mom's bedroom. I placed the box on the floor and looked around. It wasn't a huge room but it was big enough. I noticed a bathroom attached, and a good-sized closet. Not that I cared about stuff like that, but it would make Mom happy.

I left the room to check out the rest of the upstairs. I opened the next door on the same side as Mom's room: a small closet. Next, an empty bedroom. Since Matt wasn't in it, I assumed two things: it was mine, and it was smaller than the other one. Mom had told us on the way—to our great relief—that we would not have to share a bedroom. My room was cozy . . . meaning pretty small, but I didn't care, I could see and hear the ocean from it.

Across the hall was the bathroom. I opened the door and found myself in an old black-and-white movie. The bathtub stood on clawed feet and had no shower. The sink had separate hot and cold taps, and the toilet . . . well, the toilet looked like most toilets, I

3

TOM DEADY

guess that technology never advanced much. It used to be white porcelain but it was now so rust-stained it was hard to tell. The wallpaper hung in tattered strips and the room had an unidentifiable stench that I really didn't want to identify. I closed the door and walked to my brother's room. I knocked, waiting for a response. I'd made that mistake before.

"Enter," he called, in his finely-tuned Bored Teenager voice.

I stepped into the room and was immediately happy he'd picked it. It was much larger than mine, but it looked out onto the tiny backyard and the other houses beyond.

"What do you want?" he asked, without turning from his spot at the window with the crappy view.

"Nothing," I replied, trying to sound cheery. "Just checking the place out. Did you see that bathroom? How could you use it? It's nasty!"

"This whole place is nasty," he said, glumly. "And I wasn't in the bathroom."

I shrugged. "Must have been Mom. Anyway, it ain't that bad, really. I mean, the beach is cool."

He shrugged but didn't respond.

"Matt, do you think . . . " My voice hitched, the words stuck, refusing to come out.

He must have heard something in my tone, in my silence. "No, Dad isn't going to find us."

I wanted to run across the room and hug him, but that wouldn't end well for me. Instead, I just nodded. "Good."

He didn't reply.

"I'm going to get my stuff from the car," I said. I waited there a while, but he never left his post at the window.

OF MEN AND MONSTERS

I spent the next couple of hours lugging boxes into the house. The moving van arrived, adding to the chaos, but at least it looked more like a house afterward, once they were done setting up the furniture. My brother had snapped out of his morose persona and we actually had a few laughs. We found a Chinese take-out place and sat at the kitchen table eating chicken fingers and rice and a bunch of boogery-looking stuff that Mom and Matt ate but I refused to touch. We were all too tired to talk so we went to our rooms. Not exactly a *Saturday Evening Post* cover of our first night in the new house, but at least nobody got beat up.

JUNE 26, 1975

I WOKE TO the sounds of seagulls squawking and waves rolling up to the shore. I'd slept with the window open and the room smelled wonderfully salty. I bounded out of bed and leaned my head out to breathe in the sea air and look out at the beach—it was nearly empty save for a few older people taking their morning walk. I'd forgotten to plug in my alarm clock so I had no idea what time it was. With nothing better to do, I ambled down to the kitchen to see if anyone else was up.

Mom was sitting at the kitchen table, smoking, and drinking coffee. She gave me a weary smile.

"Mornin', champ. Sleep okay in the new room?"

"It was great," I replied, telling her about the sounds and smells I'd woken up to.

Her face brightened. "That's great. I think we're going to be happy here." Then her momentary brightness dimmed and I knew she was thinking about Matt.

"He'll come around," I said. "Did you sleep okay?"

She shrugged. "Pretty good, I think. It's just . . . "

I was glad she let her words trail off; I didn't want to hear anything about my father. "Do you know where the cereal is?" Even at eleven, I knew when to change the subject. I liked it when Mom smiled.

OF MEN AND MONSTERS

We both had a bowl of Corn Flakes and talked about getting the house set up properly and checking out the beach and the rest of the town. My brother joined us—well, he had a bowl of cereal, but he didn't add much to the conversation.

"What's up with that horror movie bathroom?" He asked, between mouthfuls.

Mom laughed. "Oh, I forgot to tell you about that. It's . . . out of order."

"That's an understatement," he muttered.

We could always count on Matt to accentuate the negative. I guess after what he'd been through, that was just his way of looking at things.

"The landlord said he'd get around to fixing and updating it, but probably not until the fall. He's too busy with all his other summer rentals. There's a bathroom off my bedroom and the one down here, so it's not that bad. It was part of the reason we could afford a place so close to the beach."

"One less bathroom to clean," I said. The truth is, we'd all been through a lot. Maybe because I was younger, I was more resilient. Or maybe Matt was just a grumpy teenager. Whatever the case, he kicked me under the table for my cheeriness.

"That's a great way to look at it," Mom said, pointing at me.

When she stood to put her bowl in the sink, my brother made a face and flipped me the bird. We both grinned.

Mom snuffed out her cigarette. "How about we unpack a bit while it's not too hot, grab lunch in town, then check out the beach this afternoon?

"Sounds like a plan," I said, earning another kick,

TOM DEADY

but I could tell Matt was as antsy to check out the place as I was.

It didn't take me long to get my room set up just the way I wanted it. I'd packed carefully, which made unpacking a breeze. I finished a little before noon, the final steps making sure all my books were in the right order on my shelf. When I poked my head in Matt's room, it didn't look much different than it had the night before. He was on the bed, flipping through an old comic book.

"Ready for lunch?"

He tossed the comic book on the floor and slithered off the bed. "Yeah, I'm starving, let's go see what kind of hillbillies live around here."

Mom drove through town, taking different roads than she had the night before when we'd gone to get the Chinese Food. "It's pretty deserted," I said, craning my head this way and that and finding mostly boarded-up houses.

"Bayport is mostly a summer town," Mom said. "A lot of the houses aren't winterized and the owners only use them in the summer, or they rent them out to vacationers. Most of the ones that do use the houses themselves are probably retired in Florida. Snow birds, they call them. Wait another week, this place will be jumping."

I wondered how rich you'd have to be to have two houses and never have to shovel snow. I glanced up when Mom turned the car into a sandy parking lot. The Daybreak Diner. I could almost hear my brother rolling his eyes.

"Lunch is served!" Mom hopped out of the car and bounced toward the front door. She could have been a

OF MEN AND MONSTERS

college girl in her summer dress, her blonde hair pulled back in a loose ponytail. She had a lightness in her step I hadn't seen in a long time.

I followed her in, turning to see if Matt was going to bother joining us or just mope in the car as usual. He slouched against the backrest, staring in his usual Matt way, at nothing. I followed his gaze and saw *her*. He wasn't staring at nothing, not this time. The girl was about his age, wearing tight white shorts and a bikini top. The dark brown tan on the legs and stomach made the shorts seem to glow in contrast. Even at eleven I knew she was the kind of girl who would steal your heart and your senses with just a smile. And she was smiling at Matt. Maybe she could get him out of his crabby mood. *Crabby . . . beach . . . not bad.* I followed Mom into the diner.

"Three please," Mom said to the hostess or waitress or cook . . . or probably all of the above. She turned to me, then looked around. "Where's your brother? If he's pouting in the car—"

She stopped mid-rant when I pointed out the window. Matt was leaning against the car in his best too-cool-for-school slump while the girl stood talking to him. He was a good-looking kid, tall and thin, but athletic, not skinny. His hair was long but neat and on the rare occasions he smiled, it was a good smile. Matt said something and the girl laughed, tossing her hair to the side in a practiced move. I knew that was it: she had him. "Let's sit down, Mom, okay? If he doesn't come in we can get him something to-go."

Mom looked out a moment longer and I saw her face do something weird. She looked both happy and sad at the same time. It was a look I couldn't

TOM DEADY

understand then, but which I can now recognize for what it was. Her son was growing up. Parents gets that look countless times watching their kids grow, and my mother seeing her son fall in love was one of those times. Not that Matt was even old enough to know what love was, but he probably *thought* he was in love already, just from that one burst of laughter the girl gave him.

"Good idea," Mom mumbled, following the waitress to a booth by the window.

"I'll be right with you," the waitress said, dropping a menu on the table and rushing to greet the next family that came in.

The diner had a long Formica counter with round stools covered in red vinyl. Those spinning stools were the bane of every parent: "Stop that! You're gonna fall off and split your head open!"

There were a bunch of tables and booths, also in that same red vinyl, and the floor was black-and-white checkerboard linoleum. There were advertisements hanging on nearly every inch of the wall, hawking everything from Coke to Marlboros to Gold Bond. Nowadays, a place like that would be "retro" but back then, they were everywhere.

I checked out what they had to offer, not surprised to find such New England delicacies as fish and chips, clam rolls, and Lazy Man's Lobster. Naturally, I despised seafood. But they served breakfast all day so I was in luck. I put the menu down and watched my mother. She would glance at the menu, crane her neck to try to spot my brother, then focus on the waitress, who was busy greeting new customers and rushing back to pick up orders every time someone dinged one of those bells like you see on hotel counters.

OF MEN AND MONSTERS

"Mom," I said, mostly to check to see if she was still on this planet, "what are you getting for lunch?"

She gave me a smile. "Hopefully a job." Then she stood up and walked over to the counter.

It made sense, the way she was watching the waitress. The woman was clearly overworked and frazzled. The place wasn't terribly crowded, but it was definitely too much work for one person. *Good for her*, I thought, the concept of our needing some form of income to survive having not yet crossed my mind. I watched her, the waitress, and a guy I assumed to be the cook, chatting it up at the counter. Then the waitress double-timed it over to the door to start her pattern all over again. Mom and the guy shook hands and she practically floated back to the table.

"You are looking at the new, up-and-coming waitress at the Daybreak Diner," she said with a wink.

"That's great, Mom." I held up a palm for a high-five and she slapped it clumsily. I thought about it for a minute, realizing something. "But, have you ever waitressed before?"

"Waitressing is how I got through college . . . well, the three years I finished, anyway." And in that moment, she looked twenty years younger again, like the college girl who had hustled for tips to get through college.

It was no secret that Mom and Dad had married young and that Mom had never finished college. Matt came along first, and then me. Dad worked, Mom kept house.

"I start tomorrow, working whatever shifts May can't cover. It'll be hectic, I might be working early mornings or evenings to cover the dinner shift."

She looked around again, then her eyes found mine and I saw they were glistening with tears. It hit me then just how hard this was for her. How worried she'd been about being able to take care of us by herself. This job was a huge relief for her, and it made me feel bad that I'd ever given her a hard time about moving us away. Then I got angry thinking about what a jerk my brother had been about the whole thing. I reached across the table and held her hand, something I hadn't done in years. "We'll make it work. Matt and I can help out around the house, it'll be great."

That was all it took to release the tears. She squeezed my hand back, smiling. May came over, smiling brightly, and Mom quickly wiped away the tears.

"You're a lifesaver, Paula. I was at my wits' end trying to help Chuck keep this place going." She turned to me, "And this must be Ryan."

I said hello and that it was nice to meet her. When we'd first come in, I thought she was an older lady, but now up close and looking less frazzled, I thought she might only be a few years older than Mom. We placed our orders—scrambled eggs and ham for me, a lobster roll for Mom, and a cheeseburger to-go for Matt— made small talk for a minute, then May was gone in a blur.

My brother entered the diner just as May was bringing the food to the table. He was red-faced and sweaty and had a wild look in his eyes I'd never seen before. "Mom, Kelly and a bunch of other kids are going to the beach across the street, can I go?"

I watched Mom's face carefully, curious to see her reaction. Her eyes darted to the window, as if seeing

OF MEN AND MONSTERS

these kids would be enough to determine if they were the right crowd or the axis of evil. Finally, she looked at Matt with that same "my baby's growing up" look and nodded. "Go ahead, but make sure you put suntan lotion on — and no horseplay in the water."

Matt rolled his eyes and gave me a grin. "Mom," he said, as if he was being put out somehow by her concern. I had to admit, it was about as mom-like as you could get. All she left out was the old "no swimming for at least an hour after eating" thing.

She handed him the greasy cardboard box that held a burger and fries. "You need to eat, but stay out of the water for at least an hour after." That was it. She'd gone Full-Mom.

Matt took the box, waved to us, and was gone. I must have had a goofy grin on my face because Mom said, "You know you can get cramps and drown." I burst out laughing and finished eating my eggs.

Mom and I got back to the cottage feeling full and lazy, what with the diner's food and the heat of the afternoon. She went to her room to finish unpacking and I went to mine to be bored. As much of a jerk as my brother could be, it was lonely without him; he was generally good for some entertainment. I left the bedroom, thinking it might be cooler downstairs, when that gurgling noise started coming from the bathroom again. That's when I saw it. I must have already walked past it half a dozen times without noticing, but there was a cord hanging down from the ceiling that pulled down a set of stairs to the attic. Curious, I gave it a tug

TOM DEADY

and it came down without a sound, on well-oiled hinges. I unfolded the rest of the ladder-like steps and put my foot on the first rung, then hesitated. *Better ask Mom.*

I backed up and went down the hall, calling out as I approached, "Hey, Mom, is it all right—" Apparently, her idea of unpacking was to plug a fan in, point it at the bed, and take a nap. *I tried*, I thought, and went back to the ladder. I crept up the stairs, waiting for the inevitable creaks and groans that might be enough to wake Mom, but the steps were sturdy and silent. As soon as I reached the top, the blast of hot, stale air engulfed my head. It had to be well over a hundred degrees. Still, it was worth the heat for a little adventure.

There was a pull-string directly above me and when I yanked it, a bare bulb lent dirty light to the attic space. There wasn't much to see anyway. The pitch of the roof left little walkable space. The floor itself was just a few scattered sheets of plywood. It smelled dry and somehow gamey and I wondered if there were squirrels or raccoons finding their way in. There were a couple of old chairs, a dresser with the drawers missing, and a bunch of cardboard boxes splitting at the seams. I squinted at the boxes. *Are those comic books?* I shuffled over, careful to keep my head low.

Back in Malden, my friend Timmy MacDougal had told me a story about this kid that was crawling under the farmer's porch of a house during a game of hide-and-seek and put his hand right into the guts of a dead cat. It grossed him out to the point he forgot where he was, and stood up to run. An exposed nail dug into his head and he needed a bunch of stitches and a tetanus shot. The very thought always made my legs go rubbery and I was obsessively cautious anytime I was under a porch or in a basement or attic. There were plenty of roofing nails poking through the wood above me.

I made it to the boxes with my skull intact and knelt to examine the magazines. My stomach fluttered when I realized there might be Playboy or Penthouse magazines among the contents. At eleven, I knew what they were, but I wasn't quite at the point I understood what the big deal was, though that fluttering in my gut told me I was almost there. As it turned out, there were no skin mags in the boxes, but to a kid my age, what *was* in them was an even greater treasure. Old comic books. Tons of them. Spider-Man, Superman, The Avengers, Planet of the Apes, Archie, Scary Tales, and a bunch of others I'd never heard of. I grabbed a handful and hunched back to the steps, always vigilant for those nails. At the bottom, I folded the steps away as quietly as I could and took my new-found treasure to the bedroom. The heat of the day was forgotten as I thumbed through adventure stories, some horror, and a lot of zany antics from Archie's gang.

When Mom had decided it was time to leave, *time* was one thing we didn't have a lot of. Dad was on an overnight fishing trip with his derelict buddies and Mom was still recovering from the argument they'd had about him going. It had looked like it might remain just an argument until she'd said the trip was just an excuse for him and his Neanderthal friends to

TOM DEADY

get shit-faced and bitch about their wives. She was right, of course, but violent assholes don't generally care about right and wrong. A black eye and a bleeding ear were her payback. Matt had stepped into the last few frays and ended up with minor bruises —and a lot of anger. That last fight was my first foray into my father's abuse, which ended quickly with my being thrown into a wall. I think that was the last straw for Mom. I think she always knew she couldn't protect herself from him, but the fear of being unable to protect her children, that was different.

Dad left for his trip, and we skipped town. Took everything we could fit into the station wagon and a rented truck, then got the hell out of Dodge. Remember, this was the seventies. There was no Facebook or Twitter, no Internet search engines. If someone left, they were gone, unless you hired someone to find them. The hurried exit meant we left a lot behind. Mom called it "the non-essentials," but to a nine-year-old boy, comic books don't fit that bill. I negotiated the Hardy Boys books and left the comics behind. And now, I'd stumbled upon three times as many as I'd owned, and a lot of cooler ones besides. *This is going to be all right,* I thought.

The front door opened some time later and Matt yelled up the stairs, "Mom? Ryan? Anybody home?"

I put the copy of The Avengers aside and bolted down the stairs. "You're not gonna believe what I found," I said, breathlessly.

"Your dick? You're right, I don't believe it."

My brother could be witty when he wasn't being all teenage-angsty. "Whoa," I said, "Mom is going to kill you. If that sunburn doesn't." His skin was a shade of

OF MEN AND MONSTERS

red I'd never seen on a human before. He was going to be one sorry sack later.

He just glanced down and shrugged. His eyes were wide, though, not his usual bored, sleepy-lidded expression. "It was worth it," he said, and looked me up and down. "You'll understand when you're older."

I chuckled. Matt played that card way too often, usually when he'd done something I'd never done, or he was pretending to understand something that I didn't. "Enlighten me, oh, wise one," I said with a bow. I had a pretty good vocabulary even then, or maybe I'm rewriting history to make myself sound smarter. That's the thing about memories, they can be hard to trust sometimes.

"That girl I went to the beach with, Kelly? She's . . ."

He had a faraway look in his eyes that I'd never seen but somehow knew what it meant: he was in love. At least, the fourteen-year-old version of it. I debated singing "Matt and Kelly sitting in a tree," but that was beneath me. I went for sarcasm instead. "Gee, that's terrific, Matt, when's the wedding?"

"What wedding?" Mom's sleepy voice came from the top of the stairs.

"Oh," I said loudly, staring at my brother, "while you were napping, Matt found true love on the beach and is now sworn to Kelly, till death do they part." I barely felt it when he cuffed me on the back of the head; I was having too much fun.

Mom appeared, her face puffy and her hair looking as though she'd stuck her finger in a light socket. "That's nice. Can I bring a date to the wedding?"

I cracked up. Even though the bruises hadn't faded from her last beating, Mom's sense of humor was a treat.

TOM DEADY

"You two are hilarious," Matt said haughtily, "but I don't have time for your juvenile behavior. Kelly asked me to a cook-out on the beach—" He turned to Mom, "—Her parents will be there, don't worry. Their cottage is just a ways down the beach towards town, I don't even need a ride."

Mom had finally noticed the screaming red hue of Matt's skin. "You are gonna peel like a rotten banana. What was the last thing I said to you before you left?"

Matt probably blushed, but it was impossible for his face to get any redder. "Not to swim for at least an hour after I eat. See, I listen." He scurried away before Mom could reply.

"I guess it's just you and me for dinner, kid. What are you up for?"

"Pizza and a movie?" I suggested.

Mom smiled, "Sounds delightful."

The phone rang, cutting through the house like a fire alarm. Mom's face creased as her eyes narrowed. I knew what she was thinking: *nobody has this number.* "It's probably Matt's future wife calling tell him to say she can't stand being away from him a minute longer." I raced into the kitchen and grabbed the phone. "Hello?"

I'd read a lot of books where people's blood went cold, but until that moment I didn't think it was really possible. The eerie silence on the other end of the phone made my spit dry up. "H-Hello?" I said again, this time croakier. A soft click as the person—*Dad*—on the other end hung up. "Wrong number," I called to Mom, hoping I didn't sound as close to peeing my pants as I felt.

I got a glass from the cabinet and poured myself

18

OF MEN AND MONSTERS

some cherry Kool-Aid. Remember, this was before Jim Jones, when Kool-Aid was still, well, cool. I chugged half the glass down, filled it up again, and went back to the living room. Mom looked pale and scared. "Was the last person that lived here named Farraday or Falladay or something like that? The lady that called sounded like she wanted to give them a piece of her mind." The lie came so quick and so smooth that it scared me. But seeing the stress fall away from Mom's face made it worth it.

"I'm not sure if the real-estate agent mentioned it. If she did, I don't remember. The owner's name is Howard Quinn, I know that."

I shrugged. "Ready for some pizza?"

The pepperoni pie was great but the movie was a bust. We were limited to the underwhelming choices of ABC, NBC, CBS, or PBS. Unless you count the fuzzy "UHF" channels: 38 and 56 out of Boston, which were like watching television through a blizzard. Instead, we started a jigsaw puzzle of a lake surrounded by mountains. The trees were blazing fall colors: yellows, reds, and oranges, and with the reflections in the lake, there were basically two of everything. Mom kept asking me what was wrong, and I prayed she didn't notice me glaring at the phone, willing it not to ring.

Matt rolled in around 9:30, gave a very vague "it was all right" response when Mom asked how the beach was, and trundled off to his room. I feigned a few yawns a bit later and went up myself. I knocked softly on his door, not expecting a reply. When I heard my name whispered from behind the door, I opened it slowly. Matt was sprawled on his bed, looking

TOM DEADY

ridiculous with his inflamed skin, his eyes two white marbles in a sea of red.

"You okay?" I asked.

"Better than okay, my brother."

He sounded funny, like he was half-asleep already. I walked over and sat on the edge of the bed. "The cook-out was fun? How are the kids around here?" I wanted to hear him talk more, to figure out why he sounded so weird.

He laughed, and I understood immediately. And with that understanding, an icy ball was born in my gut and started traveling north. Being my father's son, the smell of booze was unmistakable. It scared me, more than a little. More, even, than that ominous silence on the other end of the phone earlier.

"You're drunk," I finally said. I'm not sure if my voice was steady but I did manage to hold the tears at bay.

Matt laughed again, sending another wave of noxious breath in my direction. I watched him, seeing my father's face superimposed over his. I stood, and I stared. Part of me was afraid he might get up and hurt me. But most of me was just . . . *sad*. I walked out, leaving the sound of his drunken laughter behind me. When I got to my room, safe behind the closed door, the tears came.

JUNE 27, 1975

I WOKE THE next morning feeling as though I'd never slept. I remembered waking up a few times from bad dreams, but had no memory of the dreams themselves. I moved to the window, my eyes still caked with sleep and feeling groggy. *I wonder how Matt's feeling*, I thought, remembering how my dad always looked the day after. I opened the window wider than I'd left it overnight, letting the blast of cool sea air bring me fully awake. It was a picture-perfect day. The sky was a deep blue, unmarred by a single cloud. The ocean water near the shore looked greenish-blue, with the sun turning the whitecaps silvery as they crashed to the beach. Seagulls made a fuss over toward the marina, and a handful of sailboats dotted the ocean farther out, their colorful sails lending vivid contrast to the darker deep sea.

I dressed quickly and ran downstairs, not bothering to check on my brother. Mom was in her seat at the kitchen table, drinking coffee. We exchanged good mornings and I asked her if I could check out the beach.

"Sure, that's what it's there for. Be careful crossing the street—and don't wander too far."

"I won't," I replied, halfway out the door.

21

TOM DEADY

"Ryan," she called, "where's your brother? Is he going with you?"

No, Mom, he's too hungover. "I think he's still asleep, you know how teenagers are." It got the laugh I'd hoped for and I was on my way. I really didn't want to be there when she figured out he had been drinking. I crossed the street—checking both ways if only to appease my mother—and stood looking up and down the beach. Going north would take me . . . I really didn't know, the beach seemed to stretch endlessly in that direction. Heading south would bring me past the marina and eventually to town. The marina and town certainly sounded more exciting than miles of sand, so south it was.

It was already warming up. June in New England is like the joker in the deck of seasons. You sometimes get summery weather with temperatures in the eighties, but other times, the fickle hand of so-called spring clings to June with a desperate grasp. That means cool, cloudy, gray days.

That day was leaning toward what New Englanders called the "dog days"—when the temperature and humidity both raced into the nineties and you wished you were just about anywhere else on Earth. I took my time, checking out as much as I could while staying on the lookout for something cool—a shell, some pirate treasure, anything.

As I approached the marina, I remembered the seagulls I'd seen from my window flocking in this area. I scanned the beach carefully, moving closer to the incoming tide. I couldn't find any evidence of what they'd been so excited about and assumed they'd eaten it, when a wave broke in front of me, depositing . . .

OF MEN AND MONSTERS

something . . . on the wet sand. I moved closer, trying to figure out what I was looking at. I thought it was the remains of a lobster but the color was wrong and so was the shape. This thing was long, with a segmented body, but didn't have the same head as a lobster. Besides, it was bright green. It was definitely some kind of crustacean, I could tell by the armor-like exoskeleton. Unfortunately, there wasn't much else left of it to help with its identification. Another wave came, soaking me to the knees, and when it receded, it took my mysterious creature with it. I splashed into the water—I was already wet, why not—but couldn't find the thing.

Something happened, much like when I'd answered the phone and heard that ominous silence. My arms erupted in goosebumps, but not from the cold water. I was afraid. I high-stepped it out of the waves, sure that a vice-like claw was about to get my ankle. I reached the sand safely, breathing too hard. I looked down. It would be an uncomfortable stroll in sopping socks and sneakers, and just as unenviable to carry them the whole way. *And wouldn't you feel better being back in the cottage, away from the open water?* I turned back toward home to change into my flip-flops.

I heard the ruckus as I crossed the street. It wasn't Mom yelling at Matt. It was, to the vindictive side of me, even better. The downstairs bathroom was on the side of the house and the windows were open. *All* the windows were open and the sounds of Matt violently vomiting up last night's fun seemed to be pouring out all of them. I heard Mom knocking on the door and asking if he was all right. Sound sure carries around here, I thought with a smile.

TOM DEADY

I stepped in the house just as my brother was coming out of the bathroom. He looked like death warmed over, like shit on toast, like five miles of bad road, pick your idiom. And for a second, just like the night before, he looked like Dad. He might have been able to pull off the old "I ate something bad" story, but the smell oozing out of the bathroom, and likely from him as well, was unmistakable: the sour odor of old beer.

"Goddamn it, Matt," Mom said coolly. "I trusted you."

Her face was a kaleidoscope of emotions. I saw anger, hurt, fear, and confusion. But most of all, disappointment. I stood by the door, seawater pooling around my feet, waiting for his answer. He looked at Mom, and I know he saw the same look on her face, because he burst into tears.

"I'm sorry, Mom, I'll never do it again. I just wanted—"

Mom held up a hand, silencing him. "Do you know how many times I've heard that from your father?" She glared at him, glared *through* him.

Matt's mouth fell open as the tears dripped from his face. Words can take on many forms when they're used as weapons. They can cut and they can bludgeon, but they can also tear you down and make you face yourself. At that moment I realized Matt was considering his potential to be like our father, and he did not like what he was seeing. He looked away from Mom, seeing me for the first time, and crumbled into a deeper despair. Not only had he disappointed his mother, he'd embarrassed himself in front of his kid brother, becoming the thing he hated the most. He ran

OF MEN AND MONSTERS

past Mom and up the stairs, his wretched sobs echoing behind him.

Mom's protective armor cracked, and the tears came. I rushed to her and hugged her. It was all I knew to do. I didn't have any words to make it better, didn't know if those words existed. She stepped back after a moment and wiped her tears away. She was strong, my mother, and she recovered from life's disappointments quickly. She was an expert at it by then.

"What happened to you, son number two?"

I feigned shock, "Even after that, I'm still not number one?"

Mom laughed, a real, happy laugh, and gave me another hug.

"I saw something cool on the beach but a wave took it out and I followed. Ocean: 1, Ryan: 0."

Mom laughed again. "What was it? Pirate's booty? A mermaid?" Her eyes had cleared and were now bright with mischief.

"Nothing *that* cool," I said. "A weird crab or lobster-like thing, just the shell. I think the seagulls got the rest."

She scrunched up her face "I thought you said *cool*, not gross. Go on, get out of those wet things. Put your sneakers outside."

I took my sneakers off and put them in the sun to dry, then peeled off my socks. I padded upstairs, leaving wet tracks on the hard wood. The gurgling noise greeted me from behind the always-closed bathroom door—why did it always do that when I walked by? I paused at my brother's room, worried that I might hear him crying, but all was quiet. I went in my own room and grabbed one of the comic books

TOM DEADY

from the pile. The beach exploration could wait, the energy had been sucked out of me thanks to the scene downstairs. And to whatever it was that had scared me in those waves. I felt lethargic and tired. The bedroom was already hot so I took the comic book and went outside searching for a shady spot. There was a small patio in the yard with an umbrella table and some mismatched beach chairs. I found a tattered web-strap chaise lounge, positioned it in the shade, and fell onto it.

The comic book was called "They Come Out at Night," and its cover featured some kind of one-eyed bat-like creature swooping down on a scantily-clad woman. I dove in, reading the story about the monster called *Popobawa* that had been captured in Africa and shipped to the United States. The ship was wrecked in a storm off the coast of North Carolina, smashing the crate that held the beast. It flew to shore and terrorized a small town. I read the whole thing, cover to cover, only to have the story end on a cliffhanger. *There must be more of these in the attic.* The thought of going up there to find the next installment sounded good, but the heat had sapped the rest of my strength and my eyes took it upon themselves to close.

It wasn't a nightmare about a bat creature chasing me or a sea monster pulling me into the waves that woke me. It was just Mom, asking me if I wanted lunch. I blinked and wiped the sleep from my eyes just as my stomach rumbled.

"I guess that's a yes," Mom said with a smile. "I'm going to make sandwiches and see if your brother can hold something down."

I sat up, looking again at the comic book. Another

OF MEN AND MONSTERS

trip to the attic was definitely in order. A flash of red caught my eye as I stood. One foot was completely fried. As I slept, the sun must have moved beyond the umbrella's reach. *I look like an ass.* I arranged the chairs so we could enjoy lunch in the shade, as Mom and Matt came out. Mom had a tray of sandwiches and Matt carried a pitcher of lemonade and some paper cups and napkins.

"Look who's alive," she said, cheerily enough.

I knew her words were meant to poke at my brother's open wound. His expression didn't change and he remained silent. Wise move, I thought. He still looked like crap, but he'd gotten some color back, at least. Mom set us all up with ham-and-cheese sandwiches while he poured the lemonade. When Mom and I started eating, Matt sat staring at his sandwich like it was about to jump up and eat *him*. He sipped his lemonade carefully, waited—probably to see if he was going to puke it back up—then drank some more.

"Not hungry?" Mom was smiling at him but her eyes were lasers.

Matt shrugged and picked up his sandwich gently, like if he was nice to it, it might be nice back. I watched as he took a tentative bite, chewed miserably, and swallowed it like bad medicine. He put the rest of the sandwich down and went back to his drink.

"So, tell us about the cookout," Mom said. When Matt didn't respond, she added, "That wasn't a question, Matthew."

There it is, I thought, *the full name.*

"Mom, I'm sorry," he mumbled, shifting in his seat.

"I know you are. Now. But what about next time some pretty girl offers you a beer?"

My brother stared down at his plate for a long time before answering. First, he looked at me with pleading eyes, then, finally turned to Mom. "What if I'm like him?"

The horror on his face nearly made me recoil. Mom's mouth dropped open slightly, clearly expecting anything but that question. Her brows came together and deep frown lines appeared on her forehead. She looked old.

"If you keep doing what you did last night, that possibility becomes stronger each time. You might think I'm just trying to scare you, but there are studies that show alcoholism is a disease, not a choice. And like any disease, it can be hereditary." She leaned forward and took one of my brother's hands in both of hers. "You are *not* your father, but you do have some of his genetics. If you're not careful, the alcohol could get a hold of you the way it did him. And I can't – *won't* watch that happen to you."

Matt stood quickly, knocking his chair backwards, and practically fell into Mom's arms. His body shook with sobs and he wailed his apology over and over. I got up and went inside. Some things are private, and there are some things a son and little brother don't need to bear witness to.

The rest of the day was uneventful. I did take my walk on the beach, but found nothing worth writing home about. When I got back, I decided it was time to look for the next issue of "They Come Out at Night." I mentioned the comic books to Mom and she was fine

OF MEN AND MONSTERS

with me going back into the attic to look for more. She looked so sad and detached that I think I could have told her I was running away to join the circus and she would have nodded and told me to have fun.

The attic was a furnace. I rummaged through the boxes intent on finding out what happened to the *Popobawa*, ignoring the dozens—maybe hundreds—of other comics. Finally, dripping with sweat and parched, the prize was mine: five more issues of "They Come Out at Night." I put the rest of the comics neatly back into the boxes and hustled to the ladder, ever watchful for those pesky nails. As I folded the stairs away, Matt's door opened. He looked like shit. He eyed the comics I was holding, probably hoping they were *Playboys*.

"What are you doing?"

I held up my prize. "I found a bunch of old comic books in the attic. I read the first one of these and wanted to read the rest."

He reached out to me, gesturing with his fingers to hand them over. I reluctantly gave the comics over. He flipped through them, seeming interested.

"Where's the first one? I'm grounded for a while so . . ."

I smiled. Even though the *Popobawa* was a great secret, *my* secret, it would be cool to talk about it with someone. "In my room, I'll grab it for you."

Matt slunk back into his room with the first issue, and I hustled greedily to my bed to devour issue two and find out if the *Popobawa* survived the bombs the army dropped into the sewers to kill it.

By the time Mom yelled up the stairs that it was time for dinner, I was halfway through issue three and Matt had already come in to grab number two. We

TOM DEADY

both left our rooms at Mom's call and my brother smiled for once.

"Can you believe it got away through the sewers and out to that island?"

I laughed, "Wait until you see what happens the next time it finds people." His eyes widened; we were both hooked.

We ate out again that night, this time in a little Italian place in the next town. Things between Matt and Mom were civil, if a little cool, but we had some laughs and the food was pretty good. Truth be told, I couldn't wait to get home and read about *Popobawa*. The way Matt squirmed in his seat and kept looking at me, I think he was in the same boat.

"I know summer just started," Mom said abruptly, "but I have to get you both enrolled in school."

I suddenly felt nervous. Sure, I knew we'd being going to a new school in the fall, but it had seemed more like a vacation being at the cottage, not somewhere we would live, and go to school, and where we would be for the winter. A crawling fear settled in my gut, not mixing with my cheese ravioli at all. I'd be the new kid. Worse, I'd be the new kid without a father.

Mom must have sensed the mood change. "It's going to be all right, you guys. The school system here is excellent. You'll fit right in."

I frowned, the implication of Mom's words not lost on me. My brother didn't seem bothered either way. *He doesn't get it.* I ate the rest of my dinner as fast as I could, the need to get home making me panicky. Not to read comics, but to talk to Matt. I passed on dessert and waited endlessly as the others ate theirs. Finally, we headed home.

OF MEN AND MONSTERS

Matt was still grounded, so he sulked up to his room the minute we got back. Mom tried to get me to watch television, but I feigned a mighty yawn, blamed my exhaustion on the heavy Italian dinner, and went upstairs. The bathroom gurgled as I walked by, once again scaring the crap out of me. *Will I ever get used to that?* On impulse, I flung the door open and flicked on the light. Nothing save for a small puddle of water in the tub. I turned off the light and closed the door, still none the wiser.

I knocked quietly on my brother's door, slipping inside when I heard a groan that I took to be an invitation.

He was engrossed in issue two of "They Come Out at Night" when I walked in. I closed the door softly behind me.

"I'm still in solitary, Ry, you shouldn't be in here," he muttered, not bothering to look up.

"Did you *not* hear what Mom said at dinner?" He didn't lift his head but I saw his eyes flicker in my direction. "The school system here is excellent," I said, in a poor imitation of Mom's voice.

"So?" Matt put the comic book down. "What are you talking about?"

I moved closer to him, whispering, "How would Mom know about the school system here?" Don't you see? She knew we were coming here," I hissed. "She researched the schools and probably already had our report cards transferred, or whatever it is you have to do to change schools. She *planned* this." I watched the gears moving in Matt's brain.

"And the way she got the truck and found a place to live!" His eyes widened. "And where'd she get the money to even rent this place?"

TOM DEADY

In all the time I'd known something was wrong, right up until my decision to get involved and even after, Matt and I never spoke about what my father was doing. The pain he'd inflicted on Mom using both words and fists. I didn't know the word "taboo" back then, but that's what the subject was.

Matt patted the bed beside him and I trudged over, taking a seat next to him. "How long have you known? You know . . . what he was doing?"

My face burned and I suddenly felt like crying. As if talking about it made it real. Made it so I couldn't ignore it anymore. "Since my seventh birthday," I said, my voice catching as the tears came.

We were living in a little house on a dead-end street in Malden. Malden is a pretty big city but where we lived felt like a small town. Everyone knew their neighbors and hung out on their front porches in the summer. Kids played hide-and-go-seek or kickball in the streets and yards, and those same kids walked to the corner store to get milk and bread and cigarettes for their parents. Malden Square boasted the Granada Theater, three or four bowling alleys, a hobby shop that sold coins and models and all kinds of other cool stuff, and enough shops and restaurants to offer something for everyone.

My seventh birthday party was going to be held at Pleasant Lanes, a downstairs bowling alley that featured eight lanes, a few of which were almost level. Mom had reserved three lanes and had invited most of my classmates. She was going to bring pizza from DiPietro's and it was going to be the best day ever.

OF MEN AND MONSTERS

It started out great. Everyone showed up and we had a blast bowling. I got some cool presents—including the Aurora "Creature from the Black Lagoon" model—and the pizza, as always, was the best. Then my father showed up. It was no surprise to me or Mom or the other parents that he was drunk, but I'd done a pretty good job of hiding that, hiding *him* from my friends. That day, the secret was out and on full display—not just to my party but the rest of the Pleasant Lanes patrons as well. He made a big, sloppy ass of himself. I'll spare the details but the highlights were when he managed to bounce his ball into the next lane and knocked over most of the pins, and when he ran down the alley and did a belly flop into the pins, screaming, "I got a strike!" He was escorted unceremoniously off the premises and asked never to return.

All that would have been laughed off eventually. I mean, him sliding into those pins was funny. But later that night, Mom laid into him hard about embarrassing me (and her) in front of everyone. By that time, he had refined his drunkenness by downing a couple six-packs of Black Label or Narragansett or whatever cheap, shitty beer he was on then. Mom sent me and my brother to bed, but I couldn't fall asleep with them arguing. The yelling escalated and I heard the ugly sound of flesh slapping flesh. Eventually, the noise became blunter, more muffled. Punches. Then I heard sounds from their bedroom that I didn't understand.

The next day, Mom stayed in bed. When Dad went out to the bar, I snuck in to see her. Her face was a mess of bruises and she was having trouble breathing.

Dad figured out too late to only hit where the clothes covered. I think she had some broken ribs.

The kids at school teased me about Dad's antics and I laughed along with them. But inside, a sickly rage was blooming. Now I knew. Now I *watched*. I stopped talking to him and did my best to avoid him completely. Every time he hit her, that rage grew, blossoming into a pure, distilled hatred. Until one day I couldn't take it and joined the fray. And here we are.

I finished telling Matt about the party, and he nodded and put his arm around me when the sobs got the worst. It's the moment I'll always remember best about having him for a big brother.

After dinner, as if by some unspoken agreement, we all drifted to our rooms. I dove back into "They Come Out at Night" to find out what happened to *Popobawa*. There were fireworks somewhere in the distance. I went to my window but could only see the flashes in the sky, like those of faraway lightning. I finished that issue of the comic as the fireworks ended with a five-minute finale that made Bayport sound like part of a war zone.

The sudden quiet was wonderful. As my ears adjusted, the sound of gently breaking waves reached me. The night air had cooled and I slipped under the sheet. The surf had a hypnotic quality to it, and my eyes were suddenly heavy. *I'll rest for five minutes, then get the next issue.*

I dreamed I was back in Malden, waiting by the phone for my friend, Rickie Goldwater, to call. We

OF MEN AND MONSTERS

were planning on going to the movies. Finally, the phone rang and I leaped to answer it, but the receiver was stuck and I couldn't pull it from the cradle. The piercing rings were hurting my ears. I yanked with all my might and the phone came loose. I held it to my ear and heard a scream.

I came awake with a gasp, covered in sweat and wondering how fast a heart could beat before it burst like an overfilled balloon. I rubbed my eyes, thinking about Rickie Goldwater. He was a good kid but was on the pudgy side, which made him a target for the bullies. I wondered how he was doing, in that sleepy way you think about weird things. Then I heard my mother crying.

I crept out of bed and tip-toed to the hallway. There was a light on downstairs and Mom was definitely crying. No longer caring about stealth, I hurried down the steps and found her in the kitchen. She was sitting in one of the chairs, arms crossed, staring at the phone while tears ran down her face.

I realized the dream had only been partly a dream. The ringing phone was real. Probably the scream, too. And there was only one caller that could cause such a reaction. He'd found us. I ran to my mother, startling her, and fell into her arms, unable to hold back my own tears. We held each other tight. I don't know who was comforting whom, and it didn't matter.

Sometime later, I was sitting across from her at the table. "Do we have to move again?" It hit me then that I didn't want to move. All my friends were back in Malden, but somehow, in a very short time, this place had become home. Maybe it was the absence of the specter of violence that haunted the old house that

TOM DEADY

made this place feel right. It had been a bumpy start, especially for Matt, but it was getting better. *We* were getting better.

Mom shook her head defiantly. "No, honey. No more running."

I nodded, a funny warmth spreading outward from my chest. Mom was a hero. A badass. My father was the weak one. Drowning his shitty life with booze. I wondered what had gone wrong for him to end up like that. But it was a cold, clinical wonder that held no compassion. I would do anything to protect Mom from him. *Anything.*

"What are we going to do? Does he know where we are?" My brave thoughts did not translate to my voice. I sounded scared.

Mom lit a cigarette, taking a long, slow drag. She flicked a gaze toward the hall. I turned to see Matt rubbing the sleep out of his eyes.

"What's going on?" His voice was thick with sleep but held an edge of worry.

"Dad," I said.

"He found us?"

Mom blew out a puff of smoke. "He's in the process," she said calmly. "He knows we're in Bayport so it will only be a matter of time before he finds the right house."

"We're not moving," I said, my voice stronger. "Mom said no more running."

Matt moved to the table and sat. "Good," he said with a firm nod.

Mom took another drag. Her eyes were hard, staring at the wisps of smoke from the orange tip of her cigarette. "Before we moved, I checked Bayport out

OF MEN AND MONSTERS

thoroughly. The police here have a reputation for protecting women in . . . situations like mine. Like ours." She puffed thoughtfully, then tapped the butt out in the ashtray. "I went to the station when we got here and let them know what was going on. I gave them records of your father's arrests and told them it was likely he'd find us eventually. I never thought it would be this fast. I'll go back to the station tomorrow and give them an update. But, no," she turned to look at us, her expression fierce, "we're not going anywhere."

JUNE 28, 1975

THE NEXT DAY dawned overcast and brooding. I sat by my bedroom window watching the endless crashing of the waves. Sometimes, when I thought about the never-ending cycle of the tides and how long they'd been doing their dance, it overwhelmed me. The sea looked gray and foreboding under the tumultuous skies. Even the gulls' cries sounded frightened, unsure of what the gloomy day might bring.

I hadn't slept well after our family meeting at the kitchen table. Disquieting dreams plagued my night, though I couldn't remember a single one. Instead of going down to scavenge breakfast, I grabbed the next issue of "They Come Out at Night" and flopped back onto my bed. The back cover was missing, leaving torn-off, jagged edges and exposing the advertisements on the last page of the comic.

There were the usual ads for x-ray glasses and onion gum and joy buzzers and Charles Atlas, but one at the bottom caught my eye.

SEA MONSTER PETS! HATCH THESE CREATURES IF YOU DARE!

OF MEN AND MONSTERS

I'd seen ads for Sea Monkeys before, and Matt had told me they were a species of shrimp. But sea *monsters*? I read the fine print but the ad gave no details other than a legal-sounding paragraph about the company not being responsible for escaped creatures or any harm they inflicted. I looked at the cost, then jumped off the bed and grabbed my piggy bank from the bureau. I emptied the contents onto the bed and counted. I had enough money.

I cut the ad out and carefully printed my name and address, then counted out the exact amount, including shipping. I'd have to find an envelope and bug Mom for a stamp to mail it. Matt would tease me and call me a baby, so I decided this would be my secret. I slipped the form and the money under the socks in my bureau and put the rest of the money back in the piggy bank. Then I went down to get breakfast, happy with my little private adventure.

My brother was in the process of pleading with Mom to "show mercy on the error of his ways" and let him hang out with Kelly. I chuckled as I grabbed a box of cereal from the cabinet, drawing an angry look from Matt and a curious one from Mom. The quote was from issue two. I debated mentioning it, or at maybe quoting what came next, but the memory of his comforting me made me hold my tongue.

I crunched my cereal and read the back of the box while Matt negotiated his daytime beach privileges. He gave Mom a hug and bolted upstairs to get dressed.

"Hey, Mom, I want to write to Timmy and Rickie. Do you have envelopes and stamps?"

Mom smiled. "That's a great idea, Ryan. I'm sure they'd love to hear from you." She began rummaging through the kitchen drawers and pulled out a stack of envelopes. Then she grabbed her purse where a book of stamps magically appeared in her hand. *How does she know where everything is?* She put them on the table next to me and tousled my hair. "There's a mailbox on the corner on the way to town." Her face darkened. "Just for now, don't put a return address, okay? No sense in making it too easy for him."

I hadn't even thought of that, and my respect for my mother's cunning went up a few notches. "Thanks, Mom," I said, knowing I would have to write to my friends so I wouldn't be lying. But first, I needed to get my sea monsters. I slurped down the sugary milk and put my bowl in the sink. I passed Matt on the stairs. He was in a bathing suit and carrying a beach towel. He gave me a friendly punch on the shoulder as he went by. Then he turned back.

"Hey, some of the kids have younger brothers and sisters that hang out. You wanna come with me?"

I turned, waiting for the punchline. In his eyes, I had become the annoying little brother that wanted to tag along anywhere he went. He never let that happen unless Mom forced him to take me. I searched his face for a sign of malice but he looked sincere. He'd never asked me to go anywhere with him. "I have something to do first but I'll come in a while. Where are you guys gonna be?"

He glanced at the envelopes in my hand then pointed down the beach. "Not far, there's a volleyball net set up, you can't miss it."

I glanced toward the kitchen. "They're not going to be . . . you know?"

Matt looked down, shaking his head. "No, that was

stupid. Some of the parents will probably be there, anyway. You should come."

I nodded. "I will. I just need to do something." I waited for him to give me a hard time and try to wheedle out of me what it was I had to do. But he just smiled, gave me a thumbs-up, and ran out the door. I paused at the top of the stairs waiting for the nasty gurgling noise from the bathroom but it didn't come. I fished the money and the sea monster order form out of my drawer, then carefully wrote the address on the envelope. I licked a stamp and fixed it firmly to the corner of the envelope.

I threw on a bathing suit, even though the day was still cloudy, grabbed a towel, and ran downstairs. "Mom, I'm going to meet Matt at the beach," I called.

"Okay, I have to go out to pick up a few things for work tomorrow. You stay with your brother until I get back."

"I will," I yelled back, already out the door. I held the envelope tight, as if it might try to get away. The blue mailbox on the corner called to me. I reached the it just as a girl was peeking down the slot after mailing her letters. She smiled and gave me a half-wave, then headed across the street or the beach. I opened the slot and slipped the envelope in, closing it and reopening it to make sure the letter had gone down. Satisfied that my order was on the way, I crossed the street and walked down the beach toward the sound of laughing kids, the tense scene in the kitchen the night before all but forgotten.

TOM DEADY

"Thanks for inviting me to the beach," I said on my way past Matt's room.

"Wait," he called, sitting up and waving me in. "Did you have fun?"

"Are you kidding? It was great. The kids were all cool." I realized right then that we had the whole summer stretching endlessly in front of us. We could do that every day. Matt was looking at me weird. "What?"

"I saw the way you were looking at Kelly's cousin. What was her name?"

"Leah," I answered, way too fast. Matt laughed, knowing he'd tricked me. Heat rose in my face.

"Did you talk to her?" Matt wasn't laughing. He looked . . . interested.

I shrugged, wondering if it was possible for my face to spontaneously combust. "A little, toward the end of the day." I couldn't help but grin. "She asked me if I'd be back tomorrow."

"Way to go, that's my little brother," he said with pride, holding his hand up for a high five.

I slapped his palm, still grinning, face burning. We talked for a few minutes and then I headed to my own room. I wanted to get the letters written to Timmy and Rickie. It felt important, not just because I'd told Mom I'd already done it, but because I *wanted* to. The kids on the beach had seemed nice, but they weren't Timmy and Rickie.

I sat at my little desk and pulled out one of my notebooks from the year before. Finding some blank pages, I began to write. I didn't stop until my hand was cramped and my fingers had blisters. I told my friends everything, starting with what my dad did to us and

OF MEN AND MONSTERS

ending that very day at the beach. I even hinted that there was a girl I liked. The only thing I left out was the sea monsters, and I still have no idea why, but it was probably best that I did.

JULY 2, 1975

THE NEXT SEVERAL days passed in a blur, but at the same time they seemed to last forever. Mom was working crazy hours at the diner with more and more summer people—"renters" as the townies called them—showing up every day. All the boarded-up cottages were showing signs of life. By the weekend, the town would be at full capacity. Mom's schedule left me and my brother with the freedom to spend long days and some evenings on the beach with the rest of "the townies." There were a few other year-rounders besides us, but not many. A number of the kids' families owned the cottages as second homes. Others had long-term rentals, some were only there for a week at a time. Kelly's father and Leah's mother were brother and sister, and co-owned a massive cottage they'd winterized and converted to two separate units. Leah told me it had been her grandparents' place, but they'd both passed away.

On Wednesday, Mom had to cover both the lunch and dinner shifts. We'd been at the beach all day, and when the rest of the kids went home for dinner, Matt and I walked to the diner where Mom snuck us burgers and fries out the back door. We sat on an old picnic table that the cooks and waitresses used during their breaks or to grab a smoke.

OF MEN AND MONSTERS

We'd both taken to beach living like old pros. Our skin was tanned, except for my face which always seemed to be bright red or peeling. Our entire wardrobe consisted of bathing suits and flip-flops. It seemed like a chore when we had to put on a t-shirt.

"Do you ever miss Malden?" Matt asked between mouthfuls of ketchup-slathered fries.

I looked up, a little surprised at the question. His expression was unreadable.

We were pretty much living the life kids back in Malden dreamed of. Before this, we were lucky if we got to Revere Beach a couple of times in the summer. "I miss Rickie and Timmy," I answered carefully, "but not much else, I guess."

Matt nodded thoughtfully. "Don't get me wrong, I love it here. The beach is great," he grinned, "and Kelly is great, but . . . "

I wasn't sure where he was going. "But what?"

He took a bite of his burger, thinking on his answer while he chewed. "It just feels . . . temporary."

The warm summer evening felt suddenly chilly. I'd been having such a great time, I hadn't thought about . . . Dad. "You don't think we're going to have to move again, do you?" I put my burger down, no longer hungry.

Matt looked pained. *Does he know something?* "I don't know. It just seems too good to be true, you know?"

I thought of the long days on the beach, spending time with Leah, falling asleep to the hypnotic ocean sounds. Mostly I thought of how Mom had been smiling a lot lately, how happy she was without *him*. I realized I was shaking my head. I looked up at Matt, frightened for no reason other than the thought of leaving. "We're staying," I said. "There's no way we're giving this up."

Matt stared back at me for a long time, then nodded. "You're right. This isn't just for us, I mean, it *is* great for us, but," he shot a glance at the back door of the diner, "Mom needs this more than we do." He held out a hand, palm-up. "To staying," he said. I slapped him five.

"To staying," I answered.

Most of the kids were already back at the beach by the time we got there. The evening was muggy but as soon as we'd crossed the street and started walking on the sand, the ocean breeze nudged the humidity away. Sunset was still over an hour away but Kelly's parents had started piling up wood for a bonfire. The younger kids sat around holding sticks and bags of marshmallows. I found Leah with a couple of her friends.

"Do you want to walk for a while until the fire gets going?" Her friends giggled a little, looking at Leah for her answer.

She nodded, "I just have to tell my parents," and flitted away, leaving me in the awkward company of her staring pals.

"Do you like her?" One of them—her name was Mary—asked coyly.

"I know you," I said, trying to figure out from where.

She smiled. "Well, do you? Like her?"

OF MEN AND MONSTERS

I felt the flush growing in my face. I was about to stammer out some non-answer, when the conversation with Matt replayed in my head. *It just feels . . . temporary.* It hit me just how fleeting everything could be. One day we're in Malden, the next we're in Bayport. I didn't want to waste time being shy. I sure didn't want to miss out on spending time with Leah. "I like her a lot," I said with a smile. That sent the two girls scurrying away in a fit of giggles. I watched them go, still smiling. They corralled Leah on her way back and when she looked over at me, I knew they'd told her what I'd said.

"Ready to go?" I asked as she approached. She nodded and I fell in stride next to her. We walked for a while, not saying much, just enjoying the night. When we were far enough away from the crowd that her parents wouldn't be watching, I slipped my hand into hers. Her hand jerked and for a horrifying minute, I was sure she was going to pull away, but I think I just startled her and it was a reflex. She gripped my hand back and we walked on.

"You know," I said as the light of the day faded, "it was Matt that asked me to come hang out that first day. I'm really glad he did."

"Me too," she replied, squeezing my hand.

The breeze shifted, carrying a dizzying aroma of her strawberry shampoo and coconut suntan oil. I reaffirmed my vow to never leave Bayport.

The party started breaking up around ten. The little kids had devoured s'mores and the rest of us were just

TOM DEADY

hanging out, talking about whatever it was we talked about back then. A three-quarter moon had risen over the ocean, shimmering silver on the water. Occasionally a cloud would race by, obscuring it for a moment, only for it to reappear seemingly brighter.

Saying goodbye to Leah felt different. If felt final, as silly as that sounds. Matt's words echoed in my head. *It just seems too good to be true, you know?* My stomach constricted and my face and hands tingled. *What if I never see her again?* The idea was irrational but in that moment, it was terrifying. When we parted and Matt and I headed up the beach toward home, I regretted not having tried to kiss her.

"So, you and Leah are getting along, I see," he said, not in a teasing way.

His voice jarred me out of my nonsensical thoughts. "Yeah, she's great," I breathed, immediately regretting it.

"Yeah, so is Kelly," he replied, not giving me any crap about how love-struck I sounded Probably because I heard the same thing in his voice.

We got to the house and Matt stooped to pick something up. "What's this?" He mumbled, reading the box. "Hey, it's addressed to you."

I took the box, puzzled, as we went inside. I pulled the scissors out of the kitchen drawer and sliced the tape. I pulled the contents out of the box. "Sea Monster Pets!" the box exclaimed in bright red letters. I'd completely forgotten I'd ordered them.

"Sea Monkeys?" Matt said with some scorn. "Seriously?"

"Sea *Monsters*," I replied, pointing to the box. "I was bored and saw the ad in the back of one of the comics."

OF MEN AND MONSTERS

Matt took the box and turned it over, scanning the details on the back. "It's probably just another breed of shrimp," he said, handing it back to me.

"Well," I said, "the money's spent, I might as well see what they are." I opened the box and unfolded the sheet of instructions. My brother poured himself a glass of milk and watched as I filled the little plastic tank with water and poured in the two small packets. One was supposed to be the eggs, the other its food or something. I was dead tired and just wanted to go to bed.

I carried the tank upstairs, careful not to slosh it around too much, and put it on my bureau. I wanted to wait up and talk to Mom but my eyes wouldn't have it. I was asleep in no time and it wasn't tentacled sea creatures I dreamed of. It was Leah.

JULY 3, 1975

IT RAINED THE next day. It didn't just rain, it poured buckets. Real ark-building weather. At one point the wind kicked up and the huge drops flew by the windows sideways. We'd planned on hanging out at the beach in the morning, then going to a place one of the town kids knew where you could jump off a bridge at high tide. The weather had canceled all our fun. Matt and I moped around the house all morning while Mom slept in after her double the night before. She was scheduled to work the afternoon shift that day but thought she'd get cut early if the weather stayed bad.

Matt made grilled cheese sandwiches for lunch and we sat morosely in front of the television, eating and not watching whatever was on. The phone rang and I bounded out of my chair to get it, not even thinking it might be him, but Matt was faster. He talked for a few minutes, ignoring my attempts to get his attention to find out who it was. By the end of the call, he was more animated than he'd been all day. He hung up and turned to me with a grin. "Kelly's parents said she could have people over to play board games. They've got a 'great room' over the garage, whatever the hell that is, and her parents never bother her." He stood

OF MEN AND MONSTERS

next to me and threw an arm around my shoulder. "It's very private, if you catch my drift."

I caught his drift, all right, and his drift scared the crap out of me. I'd never been with a girl. It was my boldest move to hold her hand on the beach. It was my *only* move. I tried to call up my resolve from the day before, but the rain seemed to have washed that away as well. Still, what choice did I have?

We got dressed and grabbed a deck of cards and an old Monopoly game, stuffing them in a backpack along with a couple of bags of potato chips. We were about to head out when the phone rang again. I was closer this time and grabbed it, hoping it was Kelly to say plans had changed. A boring day reading comics might be better than the potential embarrassment that lay ahead for me.

"Hello?" I waited but only heard some background noise. Not static, but an engine or something. "Hello, is anyone there?"

A long sigh hissed in my ear, freezing my blood. I held the phone away from me, staring at it as if it might come alive and wrap me up like a boa constrictor.

"Are you coming, or—" Matt's eyes widened when he saw me. He grabbed the phone and slammed it down on the cradle. "Was it him?" He cried, grabbing my shoulders. "It was, wasn't it?"

I nodded, not trusting my voice to work.

"Did he say anything?"

I shook my head.

"Then how do you know it was him?" His tone was dripping with accusation.

I raised my face to his. *How could he even ask me that?* "I just know," I said, not looking away.

"Shit," he breathed, his face softening. "Okay, we already knew he had our phone number. He's just fucking with us."

"I don't know. What if he knows where we are?" As scared as I was, an ember was lit in my gut, and the more I thought about him ruining everything we had, the brighter and hotter it grew. It was rage, and within a few minutes, it was red-hot. It burned the fear out of me and made my hands shake. "Fuck him," I said through tight lips. "Let him come."

Matt looked at me as if I'd lost my mind. Maybe I had. But in that moment, if my father stepped through the door, I would have tried to kill him.

I dropped a stack of bills on the floor next to Kelly. "I'll take hotels on Connecticut Avenue, Ventnor Avenue, and Oriental Avenue," I said with a grin. "Please."

"What the heck, Matt," Leah moaned melodramatically, "you didn't tell us your brother was a real-estate tycoon."

I shrugged, scooping the green houses off the board and replacing them with the larger red hotels. "Come visit me anytime, suckers," I said gleefully.

We'd been playing board games all day, except for a short break to eat the sandwiches and chips Kelly's mom brought up to us. There were eight of us to start, but the others had gone home, some out of boredom, some after I ruthlessly eliminated them from the game.

Matt rolled the dice, then counted the spaces out, moving his car piece from spot-to-spot. He groaned, landing on Connecticut Ave.

OF MEN AND MONSTERS

"Welcome to the Ryan Arms luxury hotel," I said with a laugh. "The once meager rent of eight dollars, thanks to my vast property improvements, is now six *hundred* dollars. Cash only, please."

The girls were giggling as we all watched Matt count out his remaining cash, curse, then start flipping over property cards to mortgage them. He still came up almost a hundred dollars short. "I'm out," he said glumly, "taken to the cleaners by my little brother. How will I ever show my face at the country club again?"

"Oh," I said, taking his money and property cards, "you don't have to worry about that. Your membership has been revoked." The girls laughed as I dodged a friendly punch.

Kelly tossed her money at me. "There you go, Mr. Moneybags, I'd be out on my next turn anyway."

I looked at Leah. She was eying her stack of money and property, then looking at the board. With a shrug, she pushed all her wealth my way. "You win," she said. "I might make another turn or two, but I can't come back."

I stood and took a bow. "The top hat thanks you, and I thank you." I was *always* the top hat when I played.

We all helped sorting the money and putting the game away. "Now what?" I asked. Outside, the rain and wind lashed at the windows.

Kelly gave Matt a mischievous look, raising her eyebrows. "We could go sit on the couch and watch television," she said, gesturing to the love seat that faced the window, "and you two could just . . . "

I swallowed hard, hoping nobody had heard the

click in my throat. This was it, the moment I'd been dreading. The couch that faced the television was on the opposite side of the room from the smaller seat facing the window. It wasn't exactly private, but it was close enough.

Kelly flipped off the lights. Normally, the room would be bathed in summer sunlight, but the storm had brought a false dusk with it and the room was dark as night. Kelly grabbed Matt's hand and led him to the couch, turning on the television before sitting down.

I looked at Leah. Her hands were in the pockets of her shorts and she was staring at the floor. When she looked up, I realized with knee-wobbling relief that she was as nervous as me. In the dim light cast by the flickering television, her face was flushed. I opened my mouth to speak, became suddenly aware that I had no idea what to say, and closed it again.

This time, it was Leah that was bold. Her eyes dropped but she reached out and took my hand, leading me to the love seat. We sat down at the same time. The seat was small, but at first, we were as far apart as it would allow. Then, together, we wordlessly slipped closer.

Sheets of rain cascaded down the large bay window. The ocean was barely visible in the eerie, sickly light of the storm, but even with the howling wind, the sound of the crashing surf was louder.

I put my arm around her, unable to take my eyes from hers. Her lips twitched as if a smile was coming, but instead they parted slightly. I leaned forward. She did the same. As our lips met, I closed my eyes. Her lips were soft and warm and her hair had the scent of spring flowers. The kiss was nothing like I'd imagined

OF MEN AND MONSTERS

it. *Is any first kiss?* It's something that can't be imagined, it must be experienced. It lasted forever but was over too quickly. When we leaned back and opened our eyes, we were both smiling.

I wanted to tell her everything I'd felt in that eternity that our lips were together. Instead, I leaned in and kissed her again. It was if I had to make sure I hadn't imagined the feeling. And I hadn't, and it was just as life-changing as the first. I put my hand on her hip and she tensed.

"I pulled away, embarrassed, "I'm sorry, I—"

"No, it's not you, it's . . . " She smiled shyly, then looked over to the window. "Can I tell you something?" Her voice was barely a whisper and she was staring out at the storm. She didn't wait for a reply. "That was . . . that was the first time I've ever kissed a boy."

"Me too," I stuttered, "I mean, not that I kissed a boy, it was—" She giggled and cut me off with another kiss, this time putting her hand on my cheek. When the kiss was over, I took a deep breath. "I really like you, Leah," I said, sounding way more confident than I felt. She could ruin me with just one word, one laugh.

"I like you, too," she said softly.

If it was a movie, the rain would have stopped and the clouds would have parted, leaving a spectacular rainbow. But this was real life, and the dark clouds remained.

55

JULY 4, 1975

"HEY, CHECK THIS OUT." I stared into the little plastic tank that the "Sea Monster Pets!" were supposed to grow in. I'd slept in the day after The Kiss, and Matt and I were just bumming around in my room, reading comics. The storm had passed overnight but a cold drizzle still fell. It was supposed to clear later and we were going to meet the girls at the beach.

Matt tossed his comic book aside. "They Come Out at Night" had been a good pastime when we'd first moved in, but girls had proven to be the ultimate distraction. From everything. "Those don't look like shrimp," he said, moving next to me to squint at the tank.

Something swam in the murky water. They looked like tiny lobsters would look if their claws hadn't fully formed. Instead, ropy appendages swirled next to them, probing the sides of the tank. I sprinkled some of the food in. The creatures sped to the surface to feed. There were too many to count, but I realized with horror that there would soon be less. They were fighting over the food, attacking each other with a ferocity that was scary even for such tiny creatures.

"Holt shit," Matt whispered. "Look at the little cannibals."

OF MEN AND MONSTERS

I stared at the goings-on in the little tank, mesmerized. I'd never really expected anything to grow. And even if something did, I figured it would be like Matt said, shrimp that would float around for a few days then die and smell bad. I remembered the fine print on the form, talking about the company not being responsible for creatures that escaped or inflicted harm. I cupped my elbows in my palms, suddenly chilly. The idea of running into the bathroom and flushing them down the toilet seemed completely rational. But as scary as the little things were, they were fascinating. I sprinkled more food into the tank.

The weather didn't get better until after lunch, but as soon as it did, Matt and I were out the door. It still wasn't really a beach day, but we were eager for any opportunity to hang out with Kelly and Leah. A few of the regulars were already there, lazily hitting a volleyball back and forth over the net. The girls were nowhere to be seen.

We said our hellos to the others, trying not to seem too anxious to ask where Kelly and Leah were. Mary waved and ran over. "Hey Matt, Ryan," she said with a grin. Ever since I'd told Mary I liked Leah a lot, Mary and I had really hit it off. She was a cute girl in a sort of wholesome, girl-next-door way. Short and athletic with a spray of freckles and a pixie haircut, she seemed to have a never-ending supply of energy and conversation. If I had met her before Leah, I probably would have fallen for her. It still bothered me that she

TOM DEADY

looked so familiar, but I was stumped on where I'd seen her. "Don't worry, Kelly and Leah are just having brunch with their aunt, some weird Fourth of July tradition. They'll be back in time for the bonfire and the fireworks, don't worry.

"Thanks, Mary," I said with a grin of my own. Matt wandered off to join the kids playing volleyball. Mary and I walked toward the water.

"Leah really likes you, you know," she said, her words holding an odd tone.

"Yeah, well, the feeling is mutual, as they say."

Mary stopped, placing a hand on my arm. Her expression didn't fit the situation— it was sober, almost grim. "Just be careful, okay?"

"I don't know what you mean," I answered, genuinely confused. "What are you trying to tell me?"

Mary looked down, running a hand through her hair and kicking at the sand. "It's just . . . "

I touched her shoulder, "Hey, come on. You're making me nervous here."

Mary sighed with resignation. "She'd kill me if she knew I told you," she finally said.

"Listen, you've known her a lot longer than I have. I don't want to be responsible for coming between two friends. I don't think—"

"She was molested," Mary blurted out.

It took me a moment to process what she'd said. When the full force of it hit me, my knees unhinged and I sat down hard on the sand. Mary sat next to me.

"I'm sorry. I don't think anybody else knows. Except *him*," she added with contempt.

I was stunned, not thinking. "Him who?"

"Her father," she said softly.

OF MEN AND MONSTERS

I shook my head, the depravity of it all not sinking in. "Why are you telling me this?"

"Because she likes you, and I know you like her."

As the weight of this new information sunk in, I grew angry. "Are you trying to ruin it for us? Why wouldn't you just let her tell me?" My voice was getting higher in pitch as my anger grew hotter.

"Ryan, please," she pleaded, "she's my best friend and I would never do anything to hurt her." She picked up a small pebble and tossed it at a mussel shell a few feet away. It bounced off with a scratchy click. "I'm telling you because I know she won't," she finally breathed.

"I—"

She cut me off. "She told me you kissed her. And she told me you put a hand on her hip—"

"I wasn't trying—"

She placed a hand gently over my lips. "Please, listen, this isn't easy for me." She pulled her hand away and I nodded. "She's scared, Ryan. Not of you, just of . . . " Mary's face reddened and she picked up another pebble, rubbing it between her thumb and forefinger. "She's scared of what happens when kissing isn't enough." She tossed the pebble at the shell, missing badly.

I thought of her tensing when I'd put my hand on her hip. "Shit," I said, "*I* don't even know what happens then." I shook my head. "I guess she didn't tell you it was my first kiss?" There, it's out, I thought. I didn't realize at the time how much Mary's friendship meant.

"No, she didn't. I just assumed . . . "

I turned to her, incredulous, "You assumed what, I was some kind of stud?" It was laughable. Matt was the

TOM DEADY

good-looking one in the family. I was a scrawny kid with crooked teeth who liked comic books and sea monkeys.

She smiled. "Well, you did come across as pretty *experienced* when you told me you liked her a lot. I mean, you hardly seemed shy then . . . "

I laughed. "That was pretty much the ballsiest thing I ever did. And look what it got me. I have a *reputation*." Mary laughed, but she still sounded unsure. "What should I do?"

Mary turned to me, her face serious. "Honestly, I don't know. Just . . . be nice? If you guys . . . you know . . . start rounding the bases, and she freaks out . . . it isn't you. That's all I was trying to get to. I'm sorry I made it . . . awkward."

"It's an awkward situation," I said. "Why didn't she tell her mom? Or the police?" I wondered how I would ever be able to even look at Mr. Donovan without puking or taking a swing at him.

"I told her she should, but it only happened once." I started to say something but she held up a hand to silence me. "I know, once is all it takes. But . . . " She sighed, and it was a sigh of such magnitude and meaning that I wouldn't completely understand it for a long, long time. "Imagine if she told and everyone heard about it?"

"She didn't do anything wrong—"

The hand came up again and I shut up. I was way out of my depth anyway. "People will still talk, you *know* that. For what it's worth, he was devastated and promised it would never happen again. He was drunk . . . not that it matters or justifies anything. She just wants to move on."

OF MEN AND MONSTERS

The anger was creeping back in. Even then, I knew how this could impact her for the rest of her life. Sure, my knowledge came from books and movies, but there had to be some truth in it. "I hate him," I said through clenched teeth.

"No," Mary said sharply. "You just have to pretend you don't know. For Leah's sake." She looked at me earnestly. "Promise me, Ryan. I took a chance trusting you with this."

"I wish you hadn't," I said, more harshly than I'd meant to. "I'm sorry, I don't mean it the way it came out . . . "

"I know. I felt the same way when she told me. I almost told my parents. Sometimes, I think I should have. Or that I still should."

Something in her voice changed at that last line, and she looked down. Then, she said, "We're just kids, we shouldn't have to make these decisions. Just be good to her, okay?"

Her eyes were wet and a single tear snuck out. She swiped it away. "I promise. Being good to her is easy, and I won't say anything. Pretending I don't know when I see him, that's going to be hard." I hesitated, then the words came spilling out. "We moved here because my father hits my mother. When Matt got old enough to think he could help, my father hit *him*. When I got old enough . . . " Mary was smart enough to figure it out.

"Oh, Ryan, I had no idea. Does Leah know?"

I shook my head, blinking back the burning tears.

Mary did something so naturally and so grown-up that it made me feel much younger. She hugged me. Kids didn't hug back then, and it's a vivid memory that's stuck with me all these years. "It's not easy for me, either, knowing, I mean." She pulled away, staring out at the ocean. "Sometimes when he looks at me, I wonder if he's thinking—"

"Don't," I said, "please." I took a deep breath, letting it out slowly. "If you ever need to talk to anyone, you can talk to me." It felt right to say that, after what we'd just shared. The anger had slipped out of me, like a balloon deflating. I felt empty, sad, like part of my childhood was in the past and I could never go back.

"You're sweet, Ryan. If Leah ever dumps you, I might have to come after you."

We both laughed, but I remembered thinking how I could have fallen for her, and I wondered if she was really kidding. *What a day.*

That night on the beach was like something out of a movie. The blazing fire was surrounded by people singing, playing guitars, telling stories, and just enjoying the summer. Even my mother, exhausted from all the hours at the diner, showed up and joined in the fun. Other bonfires dotted the beach as far as the eye could see, and the water was crowded with boats anchored in the shallow water.

There was plenty of drinking, of course, and while lots of kids were sneaking beers from their parents' coolers, my brother and I stuck with Cokes. At one point, someone tried to give him a beer but he shook it off. The other kid called him a chickenshit and a pussy. Matt laughed it off for a while, but when the kid started getting louder, my brother shoved him. It

OF MEN AND MONSTERS

looked like it might come to blows, but the kid must have seen something in my brother's eyes that stopped him. They slapped palms, and that was it.

The fireworks started shortly after it was full dark. They were set off by the fire department from a platform just offshore beyond the marina. It was something, sitting there with friends and family, everyone carefree and happy. And the fireworks were incredible, I'd never seen a display like the one that night.

The only thing was . . . Leah. She'd been acting a little off since she'd gotten back from her aunt's. I asked her if anything had happened there to upset her, but she said she was fine. I asked her again later what was wrong, and she snapped "I'm fine," so I left it alone. When I kissed her goodnight after the fireworks finale, it was quick and cold, and I thought I smelled beer on her breath.

JULY 5, 1975

"Do THEY LOOK bigger to you?" I stared into the tank, trying to remember how they'd looked the other day. There were definitely fewer and I assumed the live ones were eating the dead. Maybe the stronger ones were eating the weaker of the living! The thought scared me. I sprinkled some food in and watched with fascination the frenzy that ensued.

"Shit, they are definitely bigger—and definitely meaner." Matt's voice was somewhere near awe. "Are those . . . tentacles?"

"I'm pretty sure they are. I thought they were like, claws starting to grow but . . . they're tentacles, all right." A tingling sensation started in my gut, quickly turning to teeth gnawing at me from the inside. "Do you know of any shrimp that have tentacles? Or anything besides a squid or octopus?"

"What am I, Jacques Cousteau?" Matt huffed. "There's like a billion kinds of things that live in the ocean."

One of the "sea monsters" used its tentacles to lasso another one. Then its mouth opened and it devoured the smaller one with a speed and viciousness I'd only seen once before. I imagined shark-like rows of small, needle-like teeth. *That answers my question*, I thought.

OF MEN AND MONSTERS

The year before in science class, Mr. Granger had showed us a film where a full-grown cow was stripped to the bone by a school of barracudas in less than a minute. I put a hand on my stomach as if that would ease the burning knot that lived there.

"I'm going to the beach early, you coming?" Matt asked.

"Yeah," I said distractedly, pulling my gaze away from the scene in the tank. "Leah and I might walk to town at some point but I'll go to the beach with you now."

"Cool. You two okay?" Matt's question came out slowly, tentatively.

"Great, why?" I thought back to her strange, distant behavior the night before.

He shrugged and started walking out of the room.

"Hey, tell me," I called, before he could escape.

He turned, a pained expression in his eyes. "Some of the kids were talking. They saw you hugging Mary . . ."

"We're just friends," I snapped. "What are they saying?" I stepped closer, angry. Then it hit me. Kids had been talking and Leah had heard.

"Calm down," he said, holding his hands in front of him placating me. "Just talking, that's all."

"Shit," I breathed, the anger transforming to worry. There was no way I was telling Matt *why* I'd been hugging Mary. "It's nothing, really. I'll talk to Leah today. Everything's fine between us and I want it to stay that way."

TOM DEADY

"Do you want to get an ice cream?" I asked, unsure what else to say to break the awkward silence.

Leah shrugged. "I'm not very hungry."

Wanna go to the arcade? I've got a few bucks—"

She stopped and turned to me. We were on our way to town but still walking on the sand carrying our flip-flops.

She knows. I had to make this right, and fast. "Listen, there's something I need to tell you."

"Do you like her?" Leah's voice was shaking and her face looked ready to crumble.

I shook my head, reaching for her shoulder. She pulled away with a gasp. *Shit.* "Mary is my friend. I . . . " I let out a shaky breath. "I told her about my dad."

Frown lines crossed Leah's face. "What about him?"

I was unsure of how this was going to end. "About how he used to beat my mom. And Matt. And me, once."

Leah's eyes grew wide but I swear I saw relief there. "I'm so sorry," she whispered. "I just thought . . . I mean when it was just your mom, I thought maybe your dad was dead or something."

"I wish he was," I practically growled, surprised at how intense my hatred for him had become.

She stepped closer and slipped an arm around me, resting her head on my shoulder. "You could have told me, you know."

"I know, it's just . . . " I wasn't sure how to explain it. "I didn't want you to think I was a wimp or something. I only told her because you weren't around and something had just happened. I think he knows where we are." I knuckled away a tear. "I'm afraid he's going to come here and ruin everything."

OF MEN AND MONSTERS

Leah wrapped her other arm around me and pulled me close. "It'll be okay," she said softly.

I should have been embarrassed, humiliated, but I was relieved. I held her tight and let the tears come. When we finally separated, I smiled. "This is what I was afraid would happen if I told you."

"You don't have to hide your feelings from me, you know."

"Thanks, that means a lot. Some girls might not want a crybaby for a boyfriend." The "B" word was out, hanging there between us, and I couldn't take it back. "I mean, I'd like for you to be my girlfriend."

Leah's face flushed but her smile was genuine. She put her hands on my cheeks and kissed me. Just a quick kiss—we were on a public beach—but it was enough to remind me of how soft her lips were. "I've never had a boyfriend before," she said, "and I never thought I'd have one like you."

I kissed her again, then we started walking, our hands slipping together naturally. We spent the entire day in town. Mom snuck us lunch at the back table of the diner, then we went to the arcade and finally did get our ice cream. We talked about everything from school to friends to books and even a little more about my father. I thought she'd trust me enough to tell me about her dad, but she never went near the subject. It bothered me, but at the same time, it didn't. It was hard enough for me to talk about my dad hitting me, I couldn't even imagine going through what she did, never mind telling her boyfriend about it. *Boyfriend. Girlfriend.* I liked those words.

TOM DEADY

Scattered thunderstorms rolled through the area that afternoon and continued into the evening. Mom was home from the diner and the three of us were watching television. A particularly nasty storm was going on at the time, causing the station to go intermittently fuzzy seemingly every time lightning flashed. A blinding arc of blue light exploded across the sky, followed immediately by a deafening peal of thunder that shook the house. The lights went out.

In my rational mind, I knew it was the storm. I'd heard the thunder and seen the lightning. But my first thought was, *he's found us.* I leaped to my feet and ran to the window. The entire street was dark. I breathed a shaky sigh of relief, images of my father cutting the lines to the house fading away. *Just the storm.*

"Well," Mom said tiredly, getting to her feet, "I guess that's a wrap." She shuffled into the kitchen and I heard her rummaging through the drawers, then a minute later a beam of light cut through the room. "Follow me, kids, I'll bring you to safety."

We took turns in the downstairs bathroom, then followed Mom up the stairs. I felt my way around the bedroom, finding my desk. I pulled a small penlight out of the top drawer and grabbed a comic book to read in bed. It was too early for sleep. I flipped through the issue, my eyes telling me maybe it wasn't too early after all. Just as I was dozing off, I heard a splashing sound. *Are they ever going to fix that stupid bathroom?* I heard it again, and realized it was too close to be coming from the bathroom.

OF MEN AND MONSTERS

I snapped the penlight back on and shone its weak beam around the room. *Was the roof leaking?* I got up and used the light to look for any water stains, when the sound came from right next to me. I turned on the light, already knowing what the sound was.

The beam fell on the small plastic tank and I almost dropped the light when I saw the thing staring back at me. Tentacles wavered around its reptilian-looking body, then it darted away from the light. I shone the torch around but it would always try to avoid the beam. I realized with a creeping dread that it was the only one left, and it had grown. A lot. It was the size of a small frog and bore no resemblance to the smiling creatures on the box I'd received. It was a monster.

JULY 6, 1975

I WOKE THE next day in a tangle of sweaty sheets, trying to escape something in a nightmare that was already forgotten. My first glance was toward the small plastic tank on my bureau. I could see the shape prowling back and forth even from across the room. As recent as the day before, I'd have to practically have my nose against the side of the tank to see anything.

I got out of bed and went to the tank, approaching it cautiously, as if the thing might leap out and get me. Some fragment of my dream tried to surface but didn't quite make it. Still, it gave me a chill.

The creature seemed to have grown again, even since the previous evening. It was probably two inches long but looked bigger because of the constantly swirling tentacles. I sprinkled some food in, careful to keep my hand way above the tank. It went for the flakes of dried fish or whatever the hell it was, but did so with nowhere near the frenzied enthusiasm of the past. I realized with a start that it was almost too big to stay in the little plastic tank.

I stepped away—*I'll deal with that later*—and went to the window. The storms had passed, leaving behind a perfect New England summer day. The sky was a crystalline blue so beautiful it that almost made your

OF MEN AND MONSTERS

eyes water. A gentle sea breeze carried the salty air into the room without so much as a hint of the humidity from the day before. The beach itself did not profit from the storms as the weather did. Great mounds of seaweed lay on the sand like ugly beached whales. Rocks and debris where the highest tides had reached made a sinuous line up and down the beach. The ocean itself was calm, as if it had taken a deep breath after last night's chaos.

Leah—*my girlfriend*, I thought, with a weird tingle in my gut—had a thing to go to in Gloucester. Some old friend's birthday or something. Matt and Kelly were going into town, leaving me the morning to myself. The piles of crap on the beach called to me. Perfect day for treasure hunting. I threw on a bathing suit and t-shirt, slipped into my flip-flops, and grabbed a bucket off the front porch as I busted out of the house.

It was still early, at least I thought so, based on the how deserted the beach was. Just a few old couples out walking and a pair of joggers. I realized I hadn't even looked at the clock in my haste to get to the beach.

I'd never seen anything like the things I saw that day. It wasn't just the sheer amount of stuff that had washed up, or the somehow chaotic order the waves had left it in. It was the craziness of what I saw in those piles of debris. Aside from the expected seaweed, shells, driftwood, and stones, it was as if a junkyard had been hauled to the beach and dumped in that meandering, squiggly line as far as the eye could see.

I saw license plates from at least fifteen states, car bumpers, a baby stroller, countless dolls and toys. There were street signs, golf clubs, barbecue grills, picnic baskets, pots and pans, televisions, and something that may have been a torpedo.

As fascinating as all that was, I focused on the smaller, possibly valuable items. I found coins that I couldn't identify, necklaces, almost twenty gold wedding bands, earrings, bracelets, medallions, and a diamond ring that I hoped was real. My bucket was full and almost too heavy to carry, so I had to keep switching hands, while keeping an eye on the straining plastic handle. I was about to turn around and head home when I spotted the skeletons.

I dropped the bucket, spilling my treasures back onto the sand. My first instinct was to run. Beat feet, scram. If not for the bright sunshine creating such a non-threatening setting, I would have done just that. Instead, I stepped closer. Slowly. There were two nearly complete skeletons, both with scraps of clothing stuck to the bones. I wondered how they could have ended up together after clearly being in the ocean for a long, long time. Then I saw the chain. It wasn't handcuffs exactly, but they were chained together at the wrist. Prisoner and captor, I thought. Then I studied the tattered remnants of their clothing and realized one was female. *Doomed lovers on a sinking ship who wanted to stay together forever?*

I decided it didn't matter, I had to call the police. I scooped my plunder back into the bucket and ran awkwardly toward home. Of course, the bucket's handle snapped halfway to the house and I had to pick up all the items and put them back in the bucket. For the last quarter-mile I had to run hugging the heavy bucket to my chest.

I crashed through the screen door sweaty and out of

OF MEN AND MONSTERS

breath. "Mom! Matt!" I put the bucket down, running from room to room, then up the stairs. The house was empty. There was a note on the fridge from Mom: she was at work. I assumed my brother had gone to meet Kelly. I picked up the phone and dialed the police station—luckily Mom kept all the emergency numbers thumb-tacked right above the phone in the kitchen.

Sounding like a complete lunatic, or more likely a prankster, I told the dispatcher what I'd found. They told me to stay put and they would send a car to get me and have me show the officers where the bodies were. The cruiser arrived in less than ten minutes, but it felt like ten hours. What if the skeletons were gone, washed back into their watery grave? What if someone came and took them? A dozen other irrational scenarios ran through my head. When the car pulled up, I ran off the porch.

"Are you Ryan Baxter?"

I nodded, "Yes, sir."

The officer was young— too young to be a cop. I'd expected an older guy, someone with a few hard miles on him. This kid's square face was clean-shaven to the point I wondered if he'd even started shaving yet. With bored eyes, he glanced doubtfully at the cottage. "I'm Officer Duffy. Are your parents home, son?"

Son? This kid could be my older brother. "No, sir. It's just my mom, and she's at work. At the diner," I said, pointing back up the beach.

"All right, hop in, and let's see what you found." I reached for the door handle but the cop laughed. "Sit up front, you're not under arrest or anything. Besides, I don't like kids getting used to the back seat of a police car, know what I mean?"

TOM DEADY

He winked, and I decided I liked him, even if he didn't have the grizzled look and experience I thought might be needed for this case. I ran around the car and climbed in the front seat. He waited for me to buckle my seat belt, then pointed to a silver toggle switch on the center console. "Why don't you go ahead and flip that up? We ride in style."

I did as he asked, and the bubble lights started flashing. I couldn't help but grin. He pulled out slowly, telling me to keep an eye out for the right spot. A minute later—the same distance it had taken me almost ten to cover lugging the bucket—I told him to stop. He pulled over, leaving the lights flashing, and we got out.

"Lead the way," he said.

We trudged across the dry sand until we reached the line of debris, then we walked up the beach another ten or twenty yards. "There," I said, pointing. He took the lead and approached the two skeletons. "See?" I said breathlessly, "they're chained together."

He crouched for a closer look. "Okay, I have to call this in. You did the right thing, Ryan. Most kids probably would have poked around or moved the bodies. Ever think about a career in law enforcement?" His tone was serious but he was smiling.

I shrugged. "Maybe." I glanced at his holster. The butt of his gun looked huge.

He laughed and ruffled my hair, pulling his walkie-talkie off his belt. A few minutes later, sirens sounded in the distance, growing louder until they arrived and parked behind Officer Duffy's cruiser. Soon, the beach was swarming with police officers and guys in suits. The ruckus drew a crowd like moths to a flame, but the

OF MEN AND MONSTERS

police had already hammered poles into the ground and cordoned off the area with yellow tape. And I was *inside* the tape.

I didn't know what they were all doing. There was a lot of commotion, people going over to look at the bodies, then walking around. A van skidded to a stop on the street and a pretty young woman jumped out, followed by a bearded guy carrying a large news camera. There was another commotion as the news people tried to get through the tape but the police kept them at bay. Eventually one of the men in suits, I assumed a plain clothes cop or detective, went over and spoke to the reporter. When they both turned to look at me, my heart did a weird flip thing in my chest.

A moment later, the pretty reporter was waving me over. The plain clothes cop walked in my direction. "Blondie over there wants to talk to the kid who found the bodies. Here's your fifteen minutes, pal." He gave me a wink, "Just try to look her in the eye when you're talking to her." I nodded dumbly and walked over to the reporter, ducking under the yellow police tape.

"Janice Holden, Channel Six News," the woman practically yelled. "What's your name? Can I ask you a few questions?"

"Ryan Baxter," I said dazedly, "Sure, I guess . . . "

She gestured to the cameraman, then pulled me next to her. "I'm here on Bayport Beach with Ryan Baxter, who made a gruesome discovery this morning. Tell us what happened, Ryan."

I looked at the reporter—Janice Holden—for the first time, and understood the cop's comment. She wore a green button-down blouse that she probably should have secured with one more button. It was an

75

eyeful, and I decided I might start watching the news more often. I gazed up at her face, my cheeks on fire. "Well, I saw that the storm had washed up a bunch of stuff, so I walked over to the beach to see if I could find anything cool. Then I found the, uh, skeletons," I pointed to them.

"Police on the scene are tight-lipped so far, but based on the state of the bodies, these are not recent deaths. One peculiar note: the wrists of the two bodies are chained together. It looks like we have a bit of a mystery here on Bayport Beach. I'm Janice Holden, Channel Six News." She tossed the microphone to the cameraman. "Thanks, kid. Watch the news at noon, you're famous!" She gave me a dazzling smile and trudged back on wobbly heels toward the van.

I slipped back under the tape and went to Officer Duffy. "Excuse me, do I need to stay here?"

The cop looked down, smiling. "Nah, you're free to go, Ryan. If we have any questions, we may have to talk again. Want a ride back home?"

I shook my head. "I'll walk, thank you, though."

"Thank you, son. Keep in mind what I said about law enforcement. You've got a nose for it."

I smiled and nodded, turning toward home. I was halfway home, thinking about the buttons on Janice Holden's blouse when an anvil of fear dropped on my chest. *Watch the news at noon, you're famous.* I ran, slow at first but breaking into a sprint. I had to stop the interview from being shown!

OF MEN AND MONSTERS

I crashed through the door of the diner, wild-eyed and breathless. "Mom!" Literally every head in the diner turned to look at me. My mother rushed over, probably thinking I was bleeding out or the house was burning down.

"Ryan, what's wrong?" She was giving me the once-over and patting me down like I might be holding weapons, trying to figure out where I was hurt.

"You have to call channel six before the twelve o'clock news," I blurted.

"You're not making sense."

I grabbed her by the shoulders. "I found these bodies on the beach, skeletons—" People gasped and began chattering, some getting out of their seats to look out at the beach. "They interviewed me, Mom, they're going to show it on the news." I kept my voice down but it still held the same desperate sense of urgency.

Mom got it instantly. She whipped off her apron and yelled over her shoulder, "Chuck, I gotta go, I'll be back when I can." She pulled me out the door, ignoring Chuck's bellows, and half dragged me to the car. She peeled out of the lot onto Shore Road to the sound of screeching tires and honking horns. We were at the cottage before I knew it and I was following Mom in the door. She grabbed the phone and called the operator to get the number for Channel Six News.

I glanced at the clock, a hot roiling in my gut when I saw that it was already close to eleven. Mom was talking a mile-a-minute to someone, getting louder and shriller as her face got redder and redder.

"NoNoNo, don't put me on hold . . . fuck!"

She glared at me and acid bubbled in my stomach.

It was too late. It was written all over her face. But she never gave up. She screamed and begged and cried to everyone they transferred her to. Finally, mid-sentence, she placed the receiver on the cradle softly and gave me a look I'll never forget. Then she turned on the television.

I sat in my room staring out the window, expecting my father to pull up every time I heard a car. The evening had been a disaster and I'd never felt so low. I thought Matt was going to beat me to death for my stupidity. When Mom calmed him down he just shook his head and brushed by me. Both Leah and Mary had called a bunch of times but I refused to talk to them. I have no idea what Mom had told them. I didn't care. I knew my father had already tracked us down to Bayport and had been calling, but I'd helped him pinpoint us. Thanks to my blabbering, he knew which beach we lived near, and that we were walking distance from where the skeletons had been found. It wouldn't be long before one of the cars did stop and he'd come for us. Maybe not tonight, but soon.

The tapping sound pulled me from my miserable thoughts. I thought it might be Matt knocking on the door. I wish it had been. It was the creature. It was slamming into the side of the tank, causing it to tip a little, then land. If it got any bigger—and it was already too big—it would succeed in knocking the tank over. "Shit," I muttered, not liking the fluttery way my heart was beating. I needed to find something bigger to keep the creature in. *Surely it was almost done growing?*

OF MEN AND MONSTERS

The fluttering got worse and I struggled to get air in my lungs. *Can a kid my age have a heart attack?*

I grabbed the food and dumped what was left into the water. It calmed the thing down, at least while it ate. There was nothing in my room to use, and I realized there was probably nothing in the whole house. It's not like we had a twenty-gallon aquarium laying around. I walked into the hall, about to beg for my brother's help, when the gurgling sound in the bathroom broke the quiet and solved my problem for me.

I crept down the hall and turned the knob of the bathroom, opening the door slowly in case it creaked or squealed. I flipped on the light and looked at the tub. There was a stopper hanging from a chain, but I had no idea if the water worked. Saying prayers to every benevolent being I'd ever heard of, I turned on both the hot and cold taps. After some awful banging from somewhere below me—air being forced out of the pipes, I assumed—the water began to flow. It started out a brownish-orangish color but cleared after a minute. I pushed the stopper in place, making sure the water was sort of room temperature, then ran quietly back to my room.

I stopped as soon as I crossed the threshold, my legs going rubbery. The creature had hooked a pair of its tentacles over the top rim of the tank and was pulling itself out. Forcing my body to obey me, I grabbed the tank—making sure my hands were way out of reach of those tentacles—and carried it toward the bathroom. I held it at arm's length, as if it were a ticking time-bomb that might blow any second. The creature was dangerously close to the top of the rim when I got to the bathroom. I staggered to the tub and dropped the creature in, tank and all.

It darted around the tub, tentacles swaying, checking out its new home. When the water reached about the halfway point, I turned it off. After exploring the perimeter of the tub, the creature tried climb out, but it couldn't grip the porcelain. I breathed a sigh of relief and waited for my heart to go back to something close to normal. Exhausted, I turned out the light and closed the door softly, then went to bed.

JULY 7, 1975

"**I CAN'T BELIEVE** you were on the news!" Leah was bouncing on the balls of her feet. Mary watched with a goofy grin from her lounge chair. Those skeletons, I mean—" She gave an exaggerated shudder.

I tried to shrug it off. "It was no big deal."

"Hey, what's wrong?" Leah put a hand on my arm, her excitement gone. I guess I suck at hiding my feelings.

Mary chimed in, "You okay?"

I shook my head. It was just the three of us, the others had started a game of volleyball. "I fucked up," I said flatly. "Now my father knows where we are."

"Oh, shit," Mary stood and came over to Leah and me.

"Yeah," I said, "*oh, shit* is right."

Leah's face fell. "Are you going to leave?" Her voice trembled.

I remembered the conversation I'd had with Mom and Matt when we'd decided we were staying. It was easy to be brave when we didn't really think he was coming. Now, it was only a matter of time. Hearing the sadness in Leah's voice, though, strengthened my resolve. "No," I said, surprised at how firm and steady I sounded. "We're staying."

TOM DEADY

Leah put an arm around me and rested her head on my shoulder. Mary watched me for any signs I wasn't being truthful. We were close, but her loyalty would always be to Leah first. If she thought I was lying, she'd call me out. I looked her in the eyes and gave her a nod. She smiled, but it seemed like a sad smile.

"I'm sorry I blew you both off yesterday, it was . . . I mean, I didn't—"

"We get it," Leah said softly.

"Hey," I said suddenly, "did they say anything about the bodies on the news? Like, do they know who they were?"

Mary shook her head. "No, my dad said there were tons of shipwrecks off the Massachusetts coast and the bodies could be from any of them. The storm could have shifted the wreck and . . . "

She didn't finish, but she didn't have to. I could see the battered ship sitting at the bottom of the ocean, roiling in the tempest, when a crack appears and the skeletons drift out. "Yeah," I said dreamily, "it was so weird to see them chained together like that."

"Well, at least the summer won't be boring," Leah said. "Nothing ever happens around here."

It was on the tip of my tongue to tell them about the sea creature in my bathtub, but I held back. I don't know why. Maybe I thought I had enough baggage with my father. Maybe because I was already the kid that had found the bodies on the beach.

Matt and Kelly joined us, the game breaking up as most of the kids were running for the waves. "You guys wanna swim?" Matt had been giving me the cold shoulder all morning but seemed to be loosening up.

"Last one in buys ice cream later," I yelled, and took off sprinting for the water.

"I'm sorry about the news thing, I just wasn't thinking." We were walking back from the beach as the sun was setting. Mary's parents had brought a bunch of pizzas for dinner and then built a fire. It was a mix of kids and parents and it was a lot of fun. I'd become used to spending time with Leah and sharing a goodnight kiss that it just felt normal. It wasn't until her father came to tell her it was time to go home that the subject of fathers crossed my mind. I kept my cool, though, not letting on that I knew what he was.

"It's cool. He was going to find us eventually. Part of me wants to get whatever is going to happen over with."

I thought about that as we walked. It was a dark cloud hanging over our summer. He'd probably get arrested if he showed up, and maybe our troubles would be over. *But what would he do before the police came?* I hated that little voice that always came up with the worst-case scenarios. "Hey," I almost-shouted, "I forgot to tell you something."

"What," Matt said with a smirk, "you've got your own television show?"

I laughed. "No, the sea monkey things . . . thing."

"What about it?"

We were almost to the house. "Easier if I show you."

"Holy fucking shit," Matt said, awestruck.

I'd made him wait in the hall while I opened the

door a crack just to make sure the thing hadn't escaped. When I opened the door wide enough to let him in, his jaw fell open and his eyes bugged out. "What are you gonna do with it? What if it keeps growing?"

"That reminds me, it's probably hungry. I'm out of the stuff they sent me. What should I feed it?"

"That thing looks like it will eat anything," he breathed.

"I'm going to go raid the fridge, I'll be right back."

I ran down the stairs and returned a minute later with an assortment of fruits and vegetables and some hot dogs. I noticed Matt had backed up into the hall. I stepped by him and stood near the tub, pondering what to try first. The creature stopped doing its laps around the tub and I swear it was watching me, waiting. I dropped an apple in and the creature was on it before the splash. It used its tentacles to bring it toward its mouth, then its jaws spread and I saw that its teeth had grown in deadly proportion with the rest of it. They were like shark's teeth, rows and rows of them. Then the apple was gone. I stepped back, glancing nervously at Matt. The creature floated there, waiting.

I took in a shaky breath, watching those tentacles swaying back and forth, so fluid and graceful—

"Ryan!" Matt had a deathtrap on my upper arm.

I shook my head and stepped back. I tossed the rest of the food into the tub. The creature went into a frenzy, grabbing at things with its tentacles—with I noted had some sort of hooked prongs on their underside—then tossing them away to latch onto something else. It stopped with the hot dogs,

OF MEN AND MONSTERS

devouring them savagely, almost gleefully. Matt pulled me into the hall and closed the door.

My heart was doing laps and my entire body was shaking, vibrating. "We have to get rid of that thing," I said, my voice scratchy and full of dread.

JULY 8, 1975

SCENES FROM "They Come Out at Night" played in my head as Matt and I lugged the metal tub into the house. We'd waited all morning for Mom to leave for the lunch shift at the diner, hoping against hope she wouldn't hear that thing sloshing around in the bathroom. Either that, or she'd figure out that we were waiting for her to leave, and that we must be up to something. Somehow, we got through it, and as soon as she left, we were in motion.

Along with an oversized net, the tub was easy enough to pick up at the local fishing shop, once we'd filched the money from Mom's not-so-secret hiding place where she kept her tips. The house next door had two or three young kids living there and their toys were always scattered all about the yard. We had our eye on the red wagon.

The plan was to get the creature out of the bathtub with the net, dump it into the metal tub, and hide it in the backyard until dark. Then, we would put the tub on the wagon and lug it across the street to the beach. One sea creature returned to the sea. Not exactly *Born Free*, but it'd get the thing out of our lives.

"What are you guys up to?"

I turned, and all our great plans went to shit. Mary,

OF MEN AND MONSTERS

Leah, and Kelly stood there, smiles as bright as the day itself, staring at the equipment we were wrangling through the door. *Shit.*

"Hey," I said, looking at Matt for help.

"We, uh . . . fishing, we're going deep-sea fishing . . . "

Leah and Kelly were too kind to call us out. Mary wasn't. "Cut the shit, you two. What's going on?"

Matt and I exchanged helpless, guilty glances. I sighed. "It's easier if we show you, otherwise, you'd never believe it." We forced the stuff through the door and waved the girls in. We led them upstairs, where we all stood crammed in the hall. The girls were giggling and I could only imagine what kind of nonsense they thought we were about to reveal.

"Listen," I said, in my best serious tone, "this started out as kind of a joke, out of boredom. But it's gotten out of control." The giggling had stopped and the girls were starting to look nervous. *Good.* "Just . . . " I looked again to Matt for help, but found none. "Just try not to freak out."

I cracked open the door and flipped the light on. The water in the tub was calm and I couldn't see the creature from where I was standing. I took a tentative step in, ready to get the hell out of there, and to make sure it hadn't escaped, I scanned the floor. *Maybe it's dead.* Then a tentacle swung over the side of the tub. I gasped but held my ground. Another tentacle slithered into view. "Matt," I said, "go get the fucking net. Now!"

I stayed in the doorway, ready to pull the door shut if the thing got out. The girls were all talking at the same time, their voices getting louder. I heard Matt's footsteps pounding down the stairs. "Look under my arm, you should be able to see. One at a time," I said,

TOM DEADY

keeping my voice level. "No screaming or sudden noise." My eyes never left those two oily, glistening tentacles. The chitinous hooks on the underside clinked and scraped on the porcelain as the creature held its grip.

I felt the girls changing places behind me, heard their gasps, quiet squeals, and muttering, but they seemed to be coming from miles away. My entire focus was centered on those two black appendages. Rushing back upstairs, Matt took the steps two at a time—I didn't *see* this, but I knew it. I just knew it. It was as if my senses were on steroids. I sensed him arrive next to me just as the two tentacles slithered back down into the tub.

"It's okay," I gasped, "it's back in the water." I stepped closer. It was doing peaceful laps around the tub. "Come in, slowly."

The gang huddled around me.

"What is that, an octopus? A squid? How did you catch it?"

I ushered everybody back into the hall.

"We didn't catch it. I . . . hatched it. Grew it," I shrugged. "It was from the back of a comic book. You know, like Sea Monkeys? Only these were Sea *Monsters*." I quickly told the story of hatching what I'd presumed were some kind of shrimp, all the way to my plan to release it in the ocean. I had to admit—it sounded like the ramblings of a crazy person when I said it all out loud.

"Jesus," Leah said, sounding somewhere between awestruck and terrified.

"Okay," Matt said, "we need to get that thing out of there."

OF MEN AND MONSTERS

"We need a cover for the tub," I replied, "it will climb out of that thing in no time." I tried not to shudder at the thought.

Matt was nodding his agreement. "There's an old section of picket fence out back. We can use that, it will still get air but won't be able to fit between the pickets. We can put rocks on top so it can't . . . "

He didn't finish. He didn't have to. I was already picturing those slithery, probing tentacles pushing the flimsy fence off the tub. *What would it do then?* I wondered. Would it instinctually head for the sea? Or perhaps come looking for the people who had imprisoned it? I closed my eyes and forced the images away.

"All right, let's get this over with."

It all went much easier than we expected. The creature remained almost docile as we finessed it into the net and moved it to the tub. We put the net in the tub with the creature still in it, figuring it wouldn't be able to do much as we carried the bulky tub down the stairs. Before long, we'd filled the tub with the hose and let the creature loose, securing it with the busted section of fence over it, weighted down with more rocks and bricks than were necessary, but better safe than sorry. We all stood in a circle, waiting to see what it would do. It floated lazily around, not that there was room to do much else. *Was it sick? Or could it know we were going to set it free?* As unlikely as the latter idea was, it felt right.

I dashed inside for a bunch of hot dogs and some raw hamburger to feed it with. The girls squealed when it thrashed about, grabbing the food with its hooks. Kelly screamed like a horror movie queen when she saw the rows of teeth in its maw. Then we waited. If it had been a rainy day, we could have finished it right then with the beach deserted. But it was a perfect summer day, and we'd have to wait for darkness. No way we could trundle across a crowded beach and dump that thing in the ocean.

I learned a lot about waiting that day. It can be measured in degrees. There's waiting for an important phone call, or these days an e-mail. There's waiting for test results from the doctor to see if that blood in your stool was symptomatic of ass cancer —or just hemorrhoids. There's waiting, bedside, for a loved one to pass. I've experienced all of those. That afternoon we spent waiting for the darkness to come so we could get rid of that creature, that was worse than the others by a country mile.

We were too afraid to leave the yard, the possibility that it might escape all too real. We played cards, listened to the radio, all the while keeping our eyes on the creature, but the day dragged on. It was just before dinner when the phone rang. Happy to have something to do, I bolted into the house to answer it. I knew it would be Mom, saying the diner was packed and she had to cover the dinner shift.

"Hey, Mom."

The sound that came back through the receiver wasn't even a word, just a deep breath, but I knew it was my father. Just with that sigh alone, he managed to sound amused and angry at the same time. I could almost smell the stale stench of booze through the phone.

OF MEN AND MONSTERS

Then, "I found you."

"Leave us alone!" I screamed. Then the phone clicked.

I went back out to the yard, pale and shaky, fighting back tears.

Matt was waiting there for me. He'd heard me yell and must have guessed why.

"Dad?" he asked softly.

I couldn't help it —I started crying. For a kid my age to start bawling in front of any girl was bad enough, but this was my girlfriend. And I'd already done it once. Incredibly, she came over and hugged me.

"What do we do?" I was looking at Matt, my big brother, to take control.

His eyes were wide but his jaw was set firm. "We wait until dark and get rid of this thing."

"He said he found us! What if he shows up?" I swatted the tears away and tried to sound tough.

"Then we deal with him." My brother sounded a lot tougher than me.

The waiting turned from endless boredom into the jittery feeling of a ticking time bomb. Every car I heard was my father. Every raised voice was him, coming for us. My mind was a spinning top, bouncing off one wall, dancing crazily, then spinning into another. Then a thought hit me that brought hot bile halfway up my throat.

"Matt . . . what if he goes to the diner?"

Mary stood up as soon as the words were out of my mouth. "I'll run to the diner and warn your mom."

Without thinking, I gave her a hug, and walked with her to the front of the house. I watched her go,

TOM DEADY

jogging toward town. When she passed the mailbox on the corner, I remembered that was where I'd seen her: when I'd mailed the order form for the stupid creature that was now in a tub in my backyard.

I went back to join the others. Leah gave me a look, but said nothing. Matt went into the house and returned with a baseball bat and a rolling pin. If I hadn't been so scared I would have laughed. We all sat there looking at each other, occasionally glancing at the position of the sun. I watched the tank for signs that the creature was getting restless but from what I could see between the pickets of the fence, it was only sloshing around. I considered pouring a gallon of bleach in the tank, or whatever household poison I could find, but filed it away as a bad idea. What if it didn't kill the thing, only made it mad?

More headlights flashed by on Shore Road. When I heard a car braking and saw the lights flash in the driveway, I didn't feel any fear, only resignation. I knew he would come eventually, might as well get it over with.

Matt and the girls were on their feet before me, gaping at the side of the house where the lights shone. The car idled menacingly, then the engine and the lights cut out. A door opened and slammed shut, followed by another. *Who has he brought with him?*

"Let's get inside," Matt said.

I glanced at the tank. "What about—"

"Inside, Ryan."

I went inside.

Matt told the girls to stay in the kitchen, then grabbed my arm and pulled me toward the front of the house just as the doorbell rang. I followed him to the

OF MEN AND MONSTERS

front hall, wondering why he bothered ringing the doorbell. He was more of a 'kick the door in first, ask questions later' kind of guy.

"You ready?" He asked, tightening his grip on the bat.

"Yeah." I must have sounded as weak as I felt.

He yanked open the door, raising the bat over his head—

"Whoa!"

"What the—"

It was Kelly's dad and Leah's mom.

My brother and I stuttered and blurted our way through a bunch of apologies for having almost assaulted them.

Kelly's father looked pissed, but just said, "Are the girls here?"

I noticed then how disheveled he was. He was one of those guys that usually overdressed for everything. Neatly ironed shorts and a polo shirt on the beach. Khakis and a button-down anywhere else. A preppie, in other words. This evening, he was in his beachwear collection, but it was a mess. Wrinkled, dirty, a tear in one of the sleeves of his shirt. Then I noticed his hands. They were bloody.

Matt had already called for Leah and Kelly while I was standing there gaping at Kelly's dad. He finally noticed me staring and folded his hands behind his back.

"We need to go. Now," he said, when the girls filed into the hall.

"What's wrong—"

He held up a hand. "Now!" The others all looked as stunned as I felt. The girls muttered their goodbyes

93

TOM DEADY

and followed the two adults. Leah's mom gave her a hug on the way by, and it all fell into place with an icy click. They knew. Somehow, they'd found out—or figured out—what Leah's father had done, and Kelly's dad had kicked the shit out of him. I hoped he hadn't killed him, for his own sake, not that I didn't think he deserved to die.

Matt locked the door. "What the fuck was that all about?"

I shouldered past him toward the back yard. "I'll tell you later."

We sat in silence, staring at the tank. Finally, the sun was dipping behind the houses to the west. It wouldn't be much longer before we could appropriate the neighbor's wagon and haul the tub across to the beach. I'd feel a lot better with one less thing to worry about. Then I could focus on my father.

Matt pestered me a few times about what was going on with the girls, but I deflected him. It was too much to think about. I hoped Leah was okay, and that her mom and uncle had gotten rid of her father for good. Again, I imagined the fear she must have lived with every time her father had a drink, or when she heard his footsteps coming up the stairs at night. Getting hit or even yelled at by a drunken parent was bad enough, but *that*? I pushed the thought away, glancing from the still-quiet tank to the lengthening shadows.

"It's almost time," I said.

"Thank God," Matt replied, "I can't stand much more of this. And I want to check on Kelly since you won't tell me what the fuck is going on."

I glared at him, "Kelly is fine, *what the fuck* is going on," I mimicked, "has to do with Leah. So just drop it."

OF MEN AND MONSTERS

"Fine," he said, under his breath. I think he could tell by my face that the subject wasn't up for discussion.

A while later, maybe twenty minutes, maybe two —it was impossible to tell— Matt said, "Fuck this, I'm going to get the wagon. Then we'll be ready to go at dark. Are you okay for a few minutes?"

At first, I wasn't sure whether he was talking about our father or the creature. "Sure, go ahead." Then I heard water sloshing in the tank. "Hurry, okay?"

"Back before you know it," he said, then he was gone, fading into the deepening shadows beyond the yard.

I tried to ignore the sounds that were coming from the tub, but my eyes kept returning to it, expecting a tentacle to slither out and push the fence aside. Matt was probably gone for less than five minutes, but it seemed like forever before I heard him return. We decided to wait until it was time to move before loading the tub on the wagon. No sense in riling the creature up sooner than we had to.

"I'll go grab something from the fridge to feed it after we get the tub loaded, you know, to keep it calm."

"Good idea," Matt said, watching the sun make its final descent behind the houses and trees. "It's almost *go* time."

Getting out of the yard and across the street was the easy part. Our load was fairly stable and with one of us pulling and the other making sure the tub didn't move too much, it only took a couple of minutes to reach the beach. That was when our troubles began. The weight

TOM DEADY

of the water-filled tub and the creature drove the skinny tires of the wagon into the sand. I switched places with Matt so he could pull, he was a lot stronger than me. It was still a slog. He pulled, practically leaning horizontal to use his body weight, while I pushed from the rear.

We stopped to rest and I turned to see how far we'd come. Not very. I armed sweat off my forehead. I could still see our house and it looked like a car was slowing down in front of it.

"Let's go," Matt said. "Once we reach the wet-packed sand it will be easier. It's flood tide, at least we didn't get here at low tide."

Matt was pleased with himself for learning the terms that the locals used. "Why don't you just say the tide's coming in, like normal people?"

He tossed a clump of seaweed at me and laughed.

I threw some of the food into the tub. The thing had been surprisingly calm, considering all the turbulence. I wondered if it had died, but once the food was in the water, it thrashed madly until it had eaten the lot. Then it went calm again. *It knows,* I thought. *It feels the ocean. Senses freedom.*

We continued, like Sisyphus and the boulder, until we got to the part of the beach where the tide had reached. As my brother had predicted, the work got easier. The wheels still sunk in, but not nearly as much. At last, we reached the shoreline, stopping with the wheels of the wagon in the water. I threw in the rest of the food while Matt stood, hands on knees, catching his breath. He'd done most of the work. The air was cooler right by the water's edge and the gentle sound of the sea leaving the shore was hypnotic.

OF MEN AND MONSTERS

"Well, well, well, what do we have here?"

I froze. *It can't be*, I thought, but I knew better. It can, and it was.

"If only your whore mother was here it'd be a family reunion."

His words enraged me. The slur in his speech disgusted me. The vitriol in his tone buckled my knees with fear.

He was standing about twenty yards away, silhouetted against the streetlights behind him. He was swaying, drunk.

Matt was on his feet in a heartbeat, arms straight by his side, fists clenched. "Leave us alone."

I wasn't sure my father had heard him over the surf. "Leave you alone?" He stepped closer. "I think it's *you all* that left *me* alone."

"None of us want you around," Matt shouted, "just go away!"

"Or what?" My father said, moving closer still. "You wanna try me?"

"Fuck you," I said, unable to keep the quiver out of my voice or the tears from spilling. "If it wasn't for that stupid interview you never would have found us."

"What are you talking about? It doesn't matter. I see your mother's been teaching you all her bad ways. Cussing, disrespecting your elders . . . That's another one of her problems, no discipline."

Matt was about to explode. "You don't know shit. You're a pathetic drunk who beats up women and kids. You're not even a man—"

My father charged. Just a half-dozen staggering steps and he was on my brother.

Fights in real life aren't the slick, choreographed

TOM DEADY

events they show in movies. They're ugly, sloppy, primal things. Punches were thrown and there was a lot of yelling and grunting and panting. My father was a big man, and, drunk or not, the outcome was never in doubt. He grabbed my brother by the shoulders and slammed him against the wagon. Matt's neck caught the edge of the metal tub and his head snapped awkwardly. My father grabbed him by the shirt and pulled him up. Matt's head flopped bonelessly from side-to-side until his assailant let him drop to the wet sand.

I didn't have time to shed a tear, to mourn my brother, but I knew his killer had to pay. I had the bat in my hand without realizing I'd grabbed it from the wagon. I swung hard, landing a solid blow to my father's shoulder. He stumbled forward but somehow kept his balance. When he turned to me, there was nothing in his eyes. Not rage, not murder, nothing at all. He came at me, arms up, ready to block the next blow. I swung low instead, striking his knee. The reverberation went all the way up my elbows and I dropped the bat. My father's left leg crumbled and he fell sideways against the wagon with enough force to overbalance it. The tub slid off, dumping all the water and the dark shape of the creature onto the beach.

I lurched backward, trying to watch my father and the creature at the same time, afraid to take my eyes off either. I was ankle-deep in the water, the waves beating the back of my legs. *Flood tide*, I thought. Blue strobe lights cut through the night. *Police at the house*, I thought, *but they're too late.*

My father rose shakily, a dark specter against the lunatic lights of the police car. He reeled toward me, half-dragging his left leg along for the ride. The awkward limp and the maddening lights made his approach ghastlier somehow. I could have outrun him, darted around him and to the safety of the police. Home. But I stood my ground, wishing I were still holding the bat.

He came closer, slowly. *More waiting.*

"You're gonna wish your bitch mother got the abortion I told her to," he said through clenched teeth.

More lights . . . flashlights now, dancing like fireflies up the beach. *Too far away.* Still, I didn't move.

He stopped, his face going slack, then he tipped back his head and screamed.

One of the creature's tentacles was wrapped around his good leg, and its mouth—with those rows of razor-sharp teeth—latched onto the meaty part of his thigh. He looked down, his expression a hideous combination of pain and surprise. He fell to his knees, and the tentacles gyrated like serpents before taking him in their cold embrace. He went face down in the swirling tide and the creature slithered up his body. He tried to crawl toward me, relentless in his murderous rage, until the creature's mouth found the back of his throat. His eyes found me. I'd like to think I saw regret, remorse, something in them. But they remained empty. The creature swam toward me, dragging my father's lifeless body behind it. Then it veered by me, and the monster—*monsters*—were gone.

TOM DEADY

I didn't move until the police found me, almost chest-deep in the surf. They'd been calling and calling but I don't remember hearing them. If one of their flashlight beams hadn't caught me, I might have stood there until the waves took me.

I didn't speak until they brought me home, where Mary and my mother sat with Officer Duffy, waiting. Mom shrieked when they brought me in, her eyes darting behind me, looking for my brother. She gathered me in her arms and we cried for a long time. When she finally let go, Mary took her place.

There were two or three other cops in the house, the rest still searching the beach. More sirens. An ambulance. EMTs taking my pulse and listening to my lungs and shining lights in my eyes. Always more lights.

"Son," Officer Duffy said softly, "we need to know what happened out there."

"My father killed my brother. So, I killed my father."

My mother collapsed to the floor, drawing the EMTs mercifully away from me. Mary hugged me again and I finally realized Leah wasn't there. Or Kelly. Poor Kelly.

"Okay," Duffy said, "can you tell me a little more? How did it happen?"

I felt Mary's eyes on me as I spun my tale.

"After Mary left to warn my mother, we began to get freaked out, you know? So, we grabbed a baseball bat—" I laughed, but it just made the tears come, "— and a rolling pin. He got to the house as we were crossing the street. He ch-chased us, t-to the water. I fell, and Matt stopped to help me. That's why he

OF MEN AND MONSTERS

caught us. It's all my fault." I paused, letting one of the few truths of my story sink in. Mary had my hand in a death grip. It was the only thing that gave me the strength to go on.

"My brother tried to fight him, but he was too big. Too strong. He slammed Matt into this wagon—"

Officer Duffy cut me off. "Wagon?"

One of the other officers spoke, his name was Gagnon, I would learn later. "There was a kid's wagon in the water, that's what got our attention. That's how we found you," he said.

"I think it belonged to the kid next door. Maybe he left it there by accident." Mary's grip tightened but I didn't turn to her. I couldn't. "Anyway, he slammed Matt, and his neck—" I took a breath. "His neck broke. I saw his head . . . " I gestured with my free hand, then put it back on my lap. "I grabbed the bat and hit him, hit my father. He kept coming, backing me into the water, and I kept hitting him." Bile rose in my throat but I choked it back down, savoring the pain.

"What happened next?" Officer Duffy prodded.

"Then you found me," I said, glancing at the officer who had waded in to get me. "But—"

"Take your time, son." Duffy gestured to one of the other cops and he appeared a minute later with a glass of water. I drank it greedily, soothing my burning throat.

"I think when I stopped hitting him . . . when he finally stopped coming, the water was only up to my knees."

Duffy's brow creased. He looked up at Gagnon.

"When I found him, the water was . . . " He held up a hand to just about where his badge was pinned.

TOM DEADY

"Son," Duffy went on, "is there any chance that either one of them are alive?"

I shook my head. "I don't think so. No, no way." I knew they'd never find my father's body, and hoped the sea had claimed the metal tub as well. No need trying to explain that.

"Okay, Ryan," Duffy said, kneeling in front of me. "You're a brave kid. None of this is your fault, understand?" He put his hand on my knee. And somehow, because of that small gesture of kindness, I could almost believe him.

JULY 11-12, 1975

THE DAYS OF Matt's wake and funeral were the worst of my young life. Worse than my father's abuse. Worse than all the nights I listened to my mother hurt and crying. Worse than the time he threw me against the wall. Worse, even, than watching my father kill my brother.

The police had found my brother's body shortly after I'd told Officers Duffy and Gagnon what had happened. Since he'd only been in the water a short time, the wake was open-casket. Seeing my brother made up like a wax doll in a grotesque parody of sleep was an abomination. It made me angry, not sad.

Leah came, hugged me, and said she was sorry, but she was distant, cool. Her father was not with her. Besides my mother, I felt the saddest for Kelly. She was devastated, as only a teenager losing her first love can be. She held me for a long time in the receiving line, shuddering uncontrollably. Mary showed up after Leah and Kelly, and stayed by my side. Everything had changed between the four us, but I didn't understand it, and at the time, I didn't really care.

The day of the funeral was brutally hot and humid. I sat in the stifling church in a suit that felt like heated blankets. I listened intently to the priest, searching his

TOM DEADY

words for an answer, something that would make sense of what we'd been through. I found nothing. He called my brother a sinner. It would be the last day I set foot in a church for a long time.

We arrived at the cemetery just before noon. I looked to the sky, hoping—not praying, because I no longer believed in that—for a thunderstorm to move through. It would cool things down, and besides, I thought, funerals *should* be rainy. But the only clouds were thin white wisps. My gut ached to be at the beach with my brother and the girls, that's what days like this were for.

I suffered through the graveside speech or prayers or whatever. The need to get out of there, to get away from the proximity of death, was overwhelming. Near the end, that insane part of the ritual where I had to throw a handful of dirt on my brother's coffin, I broke down. The hollow sound of the dirt hitting was too much. *What did it sound like to him*, I wondered, *from the inside?* My knees unhinged and I nearly tumbled into the open grave. My mother caught me. Because that's what mothers do.

SEPTEMBER 3, 1975

THE FIRST DAY of school had been on my mind for weeks. What kind of reception would I get as the new kid? Because I wasn't just the average new kid, I was the new kid that had found skeletons on the beach. I was the new kid whose brother was murdered. I was the new kid that had killed his own father.

I walked into homeroom, hoping to see a friendly face or two from my days at the beach, but life isn't always that kind. Sure, I recognized kids I'd seen around town or in passing at the beach, but nobody from the gang I'd gotten to know.

Mrs. Caldwell walked in and began roll call. She paused briefly at my name, and I felt the questioning eyes of a few kids, but that was all. The rest of the day was more of the same. Some curiosity, but no cringing or hostility. I sat with Mary and a few other kids from the beach at lunch. We talked about classes and teachers and how we wished summer wasn't over, normal stuff.

I walked Mary home after school and asked her if she'd heard from Leah or Kelly. I knew they'd sold the house and moved away, and that Leah's parents were getting divorced, but that was all. I'd tried calling Leah a few times after the shock of my brother's death had

TOM DEADY

had a chance to wear off a little, but she didn't want to talk to me. It had been Mary that sent an anonymous letter to both Leah's mom and Kelly's dad telling them about the abuse. I'd seen her at the mailbox the day she mailed the letter. She suspected that Leah had figured it out and that Mary and I had somehow conspired to break up her family. It didn't make sense, but grief and anger don't always lead to smart conclusions.

"Not Leah," she said, "but I finally got a letter from Kelly. She's living in Medway or Medfield or some 'M' town. She's . . . different."

"Different how?" I asked.

"She's been getting into trouble. Her parents caught her drinking. She said in her letter it's the only thing that helps her forget about Matt." She slipped her hand in mine and held it fiercely.

"Did she mention Leah?" It wasn't a touchy subject. Sure, I'd had my first kiss with Leah, but Mary and I were different. We'd kissed. A lot. But there was a kinship there that I hadn't felt with Leah. Maybe it would have been different if Leah had been able to open up to me about her father. I don't know.

"Only to say that they don't really talk anymore. She thinks Leah is angry with her. You know – because *her* dad beat up Leah's. Isn't that weird? That she even gives a shit about her father after the things he's done?"

I almost laughed because Mary never swore. She wasn't a prude or anything like that, she just didn't use that kind of language. I thought about her question, trying to feel anything but hatred for my father. "Yeah, I mean, for me, it's weird. But my father was always

106

OF MEN AND MONSTERS

the way he was, you know? I don't have any good memories of him, really. It was Mom that taught me how to ride a bike, took me fishing, all the stuff he should have done."

Mom was just a shadow of the person she'd been before Matt's death, but she was still trying. She worked at the diner and took care of the house. I helped as much as I could. I wanted her to be happy, but I feared the death of my brother, her oldest son, might never allow that. "Maybe it was different for Leah. Maybe she does have good memories and it's hard to forget those, even after what he did."

Mary stopped walking, spun to face me, and kissed me.

"What was that for?" I asked.

"Because you're a good person, Ry. I think you forget that sometimes, so I need to remind you."

"If that's how you remind me," I said, "I'll keep forgetting."

She punched my shoulder and we walked on. An ocean breeze carried the fresh scent of saltwater. It filled me with sadness and fear and longing. I hadn't gone in the water since that night, and didn't think I ever would. I knew what lurked there.

I was content with what I had on dry land.

ACKNOWLEDGEMENTS

Like many kids, I was a fan of comic books when I was growing up. I leaned more toward the "Nightmare" or "Scream" variety than the superhero comics . . . I guess that shouldn't surprise anyone. I was also drawn to the ads at the back of the comics. Things like X-Ray Vision glasses and Sea Monkeys fascinated me. Like Fox Mulder, I wanted to believe. *Of Men and Monsters* started out as a light-hearted homage to those ads. At some point, as often happens with my writing, the characters took over and turned it into something more.

First, I'd like to thank Joe Mynhardt for giving *Of Men and Monsters* a home at Crystal Lake Publishing. CLP has been on my list of favorite publishers for a while and I'm thrilled to be a part of it.

Remember that old phrase, "Don't judge a book by its cover?" I only hope the tale I've written does the cover justice in this case. Ben Baldwin captured the very heart of the story in his art, I couldn't be happier.

A huge THANK YOU to Linda Nagle, who took my manuscript and sprinkled it with red ink and magic to make the story shine.

As always, thank you to my friends in the horror writing community. So many good people out there.

Finally, I couldn't do what I do without the love and support of my family. My stories are as much theirs as they are mine.

THE END?

Not if you want to dive into more of Crystal Lake Publishing's Tales from the Darkest Depths!

Check out our amazing website and online store.
https://www.crystallakepub.com

We always have great new projects and content on the website to dive into, as well as a newsletter, behind the scenes options, social media platforms, and our own dark fiction shared-world series and our very own store. If you use the IGotMyCLPBook! coupon code in the store (at the checkout), you'll get a one-time-only 50% discount on your first eBook purchase!

Our webstore even has categories specifically for KU books, non-fiction, novels, anthologies, and of course more novellas.

ABOUT THE AUTHOR

Tom Deady's first novel, *Haven*, won the 2016 Bram Stoker Award for Superior Achievement in a First Novel. He has since published several novels, novellas, and a short story collection. Tom has several publications, including the sequel to *Eternal Darkness* and the first in his YA horror series, *The Clearing*, coming out in 2021. He has a Master's Degree in English and Creative Writing and is a member of both the Horror Writers Association and the New England Horror Writers Association.

Since its founding in August 2012, Crystal Lake Publishing has quickly become one of the world's leading publishers of Dark Fiction and Horror books in print, eBook, and audio formats.

While we strive to present only the highest quality fiction and entertainment, we also endeavour to support authors along their writing journey. We offer our time and experience in non-fiction projects, as well as author mentoring and services, at competitive prices.

With several Bram Stoker Award wins and many other wins and nominations, Crystal Lake Publishing puts integrity, honor, and respect at the forefront of our publishing operations.

We strive for each book and outreach program we spearhead to not only entertain and touch or comment on issues that affect our readers, but also to strengthen and support the Dark Fiction field and its authors.

Not only do we find and publish authors we believe are destined for greatness, but we strive to work with men and woman who endeavour to be decent human beings who care more for others than themselves, while still being hard working, driven, and passionate artists and storytellers.

Crystal Lake Publishing is and will always be a beacon of what passion and dedication, combined with overwhelming teamwork and respect, can accomplish. We endeavour to know each and every one of our readers, while building personal relationships with our authors, reviewers, bloggers, podcasters, bookstores, and libraries.

We will be as trustworthy, forthright, and transparent as any business can be, while also keeping most of the headaches away from our authors, since it's our job to solve the problems so they can stay in a creative mind. Which of course also means paying our authors.

We do not just publish books, we present to you worlds within your world, doors within your mind, from talented authors who sacrifice so much for a moment of your time.

There are some amazing small presses out there, and through collaboration and open forums we will continue to support other presses in the goal of helping authors and showing the world what quality small presses are capable of accomplishing. No one wins when a small press goes down, so we will always be there to support hardworking, legitimate presses and their authors. We don't see Crystal Lake as the best press out there, but we will always strive to be the best, strive to be the most interactive and grateful, and even blessed press around. No matter what happens over time, we will also take our mission very seriously while appreciating where we are and enjoying the journey.

What do we offer our authors that they can't do for themselves through self-publishing?

We are big supporters of self-publishing (especially hybrid publishing), if done with care, patience, and planning. However, not every author has the time or inclination to do market research, advertise, and set up book launch strategies. Although a lot of authors are successful in doing it all, strong small presses will always be there for the authors who just want to do what they do best: write.

What we offer is experience, industry knowledge, contacts and trust built up over years. And due to our strong brand and trusting fanbase, every Crystal Lake Publishing book comes with weight of respect. In time our fans begin to trust our judgment and will try a new author purely based on our support of said author.

With each launch we strive to fine-tune our approach, learn from our mistakes, and increase our reach. We continue to assure our authors that we're here for them and that we'll carry the weight of the launch and dealing with third parties while they focus on their strengths—be it writing, interviews, blogs, signings, etc.

We also offer several mentoring packages to authors that include knowledge and skills they can use in both traditional and self-publishing endeavours.

We look forward to launching many new careers.

This is what we believe in. What we stand for. This will be our legacy.

Welcome to Crystal Lake Publishing—Tales from the Darkest Depths

THANK YOU FOR PURCHASING THIS BOOK

Printed in Great Britain
by Amazon